D0018759

"These stories are not only rich in characters, events, and perceptions of the way we feel and think, they are also imaginatively written on every level, from the choice of particular words to the flow of sentences to the shape of whole stories. One sees great promise in this writer—and then one thinks, No, it isn't promise—this writer has just plain entered the city."

—Leonard Michaels

"Spence's skills in depicting the ordinary and in conveying the fragility of even the closest relationships make this a strong collection."

—*Booklist*

"The people in these stories walk that fine line between happiness and loneliness, sorrow and joy, contentment and fear. They are merely human and trying to make their way through a world that is often daunting and confusing, a world that can shift and change suddenly and without warning. In her beautiful sentences June Spence writes about them with knowledge and intelligence, with wit and insight, and a generous helping of compassion."

—Larry Brown

"Deep, rich language filled with metaphor and meaning is unquestionably one of the more stirring aspects of this collection. These stories . . . tap into and try to make sense of the hurts and pleasures common to all by virtue of simply being alive."

—*Greensboro News & Record*

"Short stories that write of life as it is, in language measured and sure. A promising debut."

—*Kirkus Reviews*

MISSING WOMEN AND OTHERS

stories by

JUNE SPENCE

RIVERHEAD BOOKS
New York

RIVERHEAD BOOKS
Published by The Berkley Publishing Group
A division of Penguin Putnam Inc.
375 Hudson Street
New York, New York 10014

"Missing Women" first appeared in *The Southern Review.*
"State of Repair" first appeared in *Puerto del Sol.* "Fight or Flight" first
appeared in *The Crescent Review.* "Isabelle and Violet Are Good
Friends" first appeared in *Seventeen* as "Isabelle (& Violet)."
"The Water Man" first appeared in *The Oxford American.*

Copyright © 1998 by June Spence
Book design by Amanda Dewey
Cover design by Lisa Amoroso
Cover photograph © by Anne Arden McDonald/Graphistock

All rights reserved. This book, or parts thereof, may not be reproduced
in any form without permission.

First Riverhead hardcover edition: July 1998
First Riverhead trade paperback edition: July 1999
Riverhead trade paperback ISBN: 1-57322-737-4

The Penguin Putnam Inc. World Wide Web site address is
http://www.penguinputnam.com

The Library of Congress has catalogued the Riverhead hardcover edition as follows:

Spence, June.
Missing women and others : stories by / June Spence.
p.   cm.
ISBN 1-57322-098-1
I. Title.
PS3569.P4454M57   1998   97-32906 CIP
813.'54—dc21

Printed in the United States of America

10   9   8   7   6   5   4   3   2   1

For my sister, Jennifer

Many thanks to
Gloria Hickock
of Helicon 9 Editions,
Leonard Michaels,
Cindy Spiegel,
and Nicole Aragi

Contents

MISSING
WOMEN
AND
OTHERS

OTHER HALVES

The couple in the other half of Fay's duplex has been gone about two weeks now. The rhythmic creaking of their lovemaking has ceased, and now the night sound is mostly faded, somber crickets. She misses the soothing racket of her neighbors. They were familiar details, if not friends. The girl played bagpipe music at six A.M. and had a pleasant, horsey smell. The guy had no muffler in his jeep and often left his mud-caked thongs out to dry on the front porch. Fay is wondering where they went, why.

She has never been so interested in anyone's business before now. Alone, she pays attention to the background noises. More is at stake. A rustle at the window, and she listens for distinctions: unintentional, the wind at the branches again, or deliberate, a hand parting the brush.

When the front door swelled from the heat a few nights ago, Fay couldn't push it shut enough to make the bolt click locked. With Cliff around, she'd have just put on the chain and gone to bed. But she sensed how fragile the chain was, how just a shoulder braced against the door could snap it. She slept in the foyer that night, ready to greet the intruder right off.

Evenings alone are sometimes more difficult than Fay would like to admit. A little wine tends to soften this knowledge and make the night noises less interesting. Fay usually buys Chablis or Rhine in two- or three-liter jugs for greater economy. She prides herself at how long it took to finish the last bottle at the rate of one or two glasses a day: two and a half weeks. She figures this surely is a normal rate of consumption for a single person. She paces herself by taking occasional delicate sips. She traces up the stem of her glass, cups the bulb in her palm, lifts it slowly to her lips, tips the cold, tart liquid gently into her mouth.

Drinking must remain a deliberate act, she feels. Developing and adhering to new routines, certainties to rely on, has been a nice distraction for Fay. Breakfast is always an apple or a pear, a glass of tea, and two Dexatrims. She enjoys the anxious spurts that the capsules send thrilling through her veins all day. They don't seem to break her appetite; by lunch she is usually hungry for a cheeseburger, fries drenched in gravy, and a salad with blue cheese dressing. Dinner is the cautious intake of wine.

She has tried to explain this to Cliff, how it illustrates the control she has begun to exert over her actions. He appears to be listening, but his response is then to ask about the car or whether she needs money. He stops over now only to pick up leftover items: a tire iron, his aftershave, the jacket with suede elbow patches. He cannot stay long; a tic begins to pulse at the corner of his mouth, curling it into a snarl.

Fay considers it bad sportsmanship on his part. After all, she stayed with him and was faithful for a full year after he tore up her car and slapped a bruise on her cheek, six months after he was rumored to be dating the seventeen-year-old waitress at Captain Nemo's. These things had pissed her off, of course, but she was slowly deadening to them. Then Lou.

Lou had gotten apprenticed to Fay's uncle Bert shortly after the Cliff-waitress talk began. Bert, a crusty old sign painter, whose hand was still true but whose eyesight was going fast, was glad to have him. Bert wanted someone to pass on the business to, since his own uninterested children had gone into banking, used-car sales, and prison. Lou was an art school dropout with a care for detail and an eye for color that gladdened Bert's heart.

Before Fay got the accounting job at Fritzi's Junior College, which offered medical insurance, she kept the books at Bert's shop and ran the vinyl letter cutter that he never quite got the hang of. She had made a point of not talking too much to Lou when he was first hired; her suspicions of Cliff still made her crave revenge sometimes, so she felt it dangerous to get to know any new men. Still, she watched with interest as he learned the rudiments of sign painting. Bert had eaten apprentices for breakfast for a good two years before Lou. Fay lost count of how many had broken under Bert's rasping criticism. She was ready for the day that Lou would be driven cursing from the shop.

Curiously, Lou lingered on, undaunted by the abrasive instruction he was given.

"You call that blob an oval?" Bert would taunt. "I said *serifs*, not tree branches sprouting off the goddamn letters. Give me a good clean Times, not some psychedelic hippyshit." Lou might snort in appreciation or shift to get a better angle on the board, but he never wavered in his gaze, never stopped painting. Bert's razzing began to take on a more affectionate tone.

"Look at that crazy sonofabitch," he'd tell Fay, palming the greasy shock of white hair off his forehead. "Works his sorry ass off for six an hour and no benefits. Look at him! Barely even pencils in his designs. Fucking Rembrandt up there!"

And Fay looked. No harm in that. Only there was such focused power in his stance, the sweeps and arcs of his arms, his wrists, the fluid motions of his hands. She'd never seen a more deliberate man. Fay began to ponder what all else those graceful, capable hands could do, and found she could barely look him in the eye after that. *I am married*, she told herself often, but that only underlined the fact that she needed to be touched with some skill.

Lou's and Fay's birthday fell within a few days of each other, so Bert brought a cake to the shop. It had *Happy Birthday Fay* written in pink cursive frosting, with *& Lou* added in blue. Bert is an economical man. If two birthdays could be covered with one cake, then so much the better. Now he feels somewhat responsible, as if by pairing them on the cake he set something inexorable in motion.

In a way, he did. The very notion of sharing a birthday cake with Lou, their breaths mingling over the blown-out candles, proved too much for Fay. She devoured the mealy white cake. When Lou leaned over and gently brushed a glob of frosting off her chin, something inside her just shifted out of place.

That oddness inside still remains, keeps her perpetually dissatisfied. She surveys her half of the little duplex: the bad gold rug, her carefully framed seascapes on the walls, Cliff's extravagant big-screen TV, which takes up so much space. She despairs at how all the furniture slants expectantly toward it. She doubts the couple next door even has a television. She has never heard the dim murmuring through the walls, never glimpsed a pulsating glow through their windows when she came home late.

She has heard their most intimate sounds, though, and wonders what they might have heard from her. She remembers one night when she was unable to keep from yelling at Cliff. Her tirade was incomprehensible to him, something about skilled hands versus hands that slap, hands that touch other women. "Which do you think I have chosen?" she shouted imperiously. But he simply had no idea yet what or whom she meant. How much did they know?

But the couple is not here to be asked, and Cliff is no longer around to fuel her anger by shrugging helplessly at it. Fay takes a measured gulp from her glass and ponders her next move. Once she would have gargled, changed panties, run a brush through her hair, and headed back over to the shop. Lou would be there even now, probably, practicing his curlicues, airbrushing shaded spheres onto scraps of resin board.

That first night she went, she found him straddling a bench with a pint of whiskey, quietly regarding a steer-shaped sign Bert had left him to finish. *Sample Sadie's Succulent Sirloin*, it read. *Exit 22 miles.* The letters were painted a raw-meat red, streaked white with fat. Fay had come to talk to him but had some leftover paperwork to finish in case she lost her nerve.

He greeted Fay with a surprised smile, then gestured at the sign for her opinion.

"Gross," she offered. "But . . . technically brilliant?"

"Story of my life." He sighed, offering her the bottle.

Fay sat next to him on the bench and took a long swig. It made a good burn down her throat. She thought if she could just break down and cry, he'd have to comfort her. But she felt too happy. She said to herself, *My marriage is wrecked*; sometimes that thought would cause tears to well up. But now it just made her giddy with desire. She tried it aloud: "My marriage is wrecked." She felt her face smirking around the words. "Oh God," she cried, covering her face with her hands, too late to conceal the laughter erupting from her.

She shook with it for a few moments. Lou, bewildered, sipped the whiskey in silence. When she had quieted down some, he handed her back the bottle. She took another long pull and felt her face and chest flush.

"My marriage," she said, "is wrecked." She snorted, giggled, howled with laughter. She reached again for the bottle.

"Good Christ," said Lou. "Drink up."

"You have such nice hands," she told him, laughter suddenly gone. She touched his wrist lightly, then pulled back, frightened.

"It's all right," he said. "Come here." And with those deft, gentle hands, then the length of his body, he drew her in.

There had been a brief period of halfhearted subterfuge before Cliff found out. Fay might say carelessly to him, "I'm out with the girls tonight," as she left, or, "Late night at the shop," as she came in. Barely adequate, but they went unchallenged. Soon she dispensed with even the lamest excuses, just came and went.

Then Fay drifted in one morning about three A.M. She wriggled out of her bra, peeled off her panties, glimpsed herself in the dresser mirror, her body contoured by moonlight. Another shape loomed in the reflection, and she whirled around. It was Cliff, sitting straight up in bed.

She got that caught feeling, of course, but like at age six, standing before her mother, who asked her, "Were you eating candy?" and though she was sticky with it, hands, face, hair, the lie spilled easily from her mouth. So she was then, sticky with evidence: face and neck scraped raw by Lou's stubble, dried and peeling spots on her breasts and stomach, and the lie spilled easily from her mouth.

It wasn't so much her sleeping with Lou but the consummate ease with which she did it that angered him most. Cliff threw some clothing into a gym bag and left; Fay slept like a sated baby.

She longs for that easy sleep now. But with night coming and no word yet from Lou, she is coiled tight, expectant. There is no rule that says he will come, that she will even hear from him, but something prevents her from seeking him out instead.

Not pride, exactly, but she tallies his advances and hers, tries to keep them even.

The girth of him, the fit. It is as though her body has been indelibly molded by his. The curve of her cheek conforms to the nape of his neck; her belly presses flush against the small of his back when they sleep like spoons. They shift and relink in endless combinations, multiplied, the sum of parts: a shoulder wedging into an armpit, hair meshing, palms cupping hips, buttocks, the soft thudding of pelvic bones, nails dancing down a spine, a tongue glistening a nipple erect, breath caressing hollows, the dip between breasts, the navel, tickly parting hairs, working slowly into the warmth, the clasping, the tugging in.

When she runs into Lou around town, it is as though this never was. He greets her with a curt nod, if at all. It is like getting punched in the stomach, this public denial. She wants to tell him how she gave up everything for him, but in truth she lost little or nothing. The old constancy, perhaps. The deadening feeling. And he never asked her to, anyway.

It grows late, and Fay feels with grim certainty that there will be no call, no visit, tonight. The house feels hollow, silent, in need of blotting out, but Fay empties her wineglass into the toilet and turns out the lights.

A sputtering, mufflerless jeep careens into the driveway, its headlights illuminating her bedroom for a swift moment. The neighbors are back, Fay realizes with delight. She pauses in the doorway of her bedroom, relishing the door slams, the familiar clapping of his thongs, the crunching of her boots on gravel as they approach the house. They enter and their footfalls become soft wooden creakings that quickly fade into silence.

She undresses slowly, deliberately, then stretches out on top of the bedcovers. It is as though she is unwilling to penetrate that layer of down without damn good reason. After Lou stays over, the bed takes on a ravaged, haggard look: the pillows are flung away, the sheets and pad wrenched back to expose striped, stained ticking. It is small consolation that the bed will require only a light smoothing tomorrow morning.

Fay listens hard, hoping to be lulled by the neighbors' sounds, but the house has settled and grown still again. They must be tired from a long trip. She imagines them lying together, their bodies linked and quiet in the dark, and for now it is enough. She pats the empty space beside her and lets the trees whisper her to sleep.

A Nice Man, A Good Girl

Emile does sometimes, idly, consider his alternate life, add eighteen years to the day his baby might have made it to birth alive, blood illuminating the skin. Her skin, a daughter. Assuming no other mishaps occurred, by this time he might have watched her graduate high school, hauled her possessions to a college dormitory in a nearby city, walked her down the aisle—any number of touching fatherly things. Her face is an amalgamation of Emile's and her mother's, so her eyes are his, sharp, her nose and the curve of her cheeks have a familiar tilt but vague; he hasn't seen her mother, his ex-wife, in more than a decade.

This isn't something he dwells on too often. It was a long time ago, and though the loss was of course tragic, he senses only undertones of guilt and relief, glimpses of a baroque toy casket. But he adds, nonetheless. Eighteen years to the machine shop where he might yet be, assuming no layoffs occurred, or if they did, some other venue for a young, honorably discharged soldier with a new wife and kid. Or perhaps he would have opted to stay in the military. That plus eighteen years would have equaled what? Instead of now, his life in a rental house, funky and remote, full of stray animals; his liberal arts degree serving only decorative purposes in its hand-painted frame while he conducts tours and tastings at the winery; his state-of-the-art bicycle and stereo system; a diverse and fascinating string of lovers, their bodies, various and pliant, now open only to his reminiscences. He has worked hard, nonetheless, without the wife and kid. His hands bear the same thickened ovals of callus they would have, only these were acquired in an assortment of jobs and places, with interims between for travel, for reassessments. Luxuries he would likely not have had.

His parents would define his present state as an interim, certainly, though he would not. They quibble over the use of terms. *Success*, for example, has markedly different connotations for him than for them. He accepts this and knows they do too, despite their ritual indications of displeasure on holidays. And they are fond of Penny, though less fond that she is moving in with Emile, because this they have seen before. It is the kind of thing that can drag on for years without producing a marriage or children, nothing they can claim as partly theirs. The living situation only compromises his already infrequent visits—gain with no payoff, because they can't say, *Emile's with his in-laws*. It just appears as if he'd rather be with somebody else's parents.

This may be true, but only because Penny's parents are closer to his age and fairly enthused about his plans. Over icy gin drinks, they conspire mildly in Penny's absence over her future. She was named Judith but since the Girl Scouts has answered only to Penny, for her middle name, Penelope, and for her copper-colored hair. There is a budding campaign to coax her back to her original name, and Emile intends to participate in a teasing way. "Hey, Jude," he plans to greet her in singsong fashion when she arrives from work, knowing she will stare humorlessly at each of them in turn before dismissing them with, "That just doesn't even *sound* like me." Penny will then express admiration for the cut-glass pitcher of lemonade as she pours herself a drink and douses it with gin. Her father, Stu, will gas up the grill for salmon and ribs, and Emile and Penny will eat until they are swollen and tired, a way they rarely eat on their own. As they are preparing to leave, her mother, Daphne, will wrap up the leftovers to send back with them and present Penny with the pitcher as a gift. Penny will refuse and her mother will insist and there will be a petty, affectionate squabble at the door before Emile swoops down and accepts the pitcher, saying thank you, thank you, for *everything*, and her parents will look back at him meaningfully because they know he is referring to those moments just before their daughter arrived, when they agreed to lend him five thousand dollars—which is why he has come to their house early, before Penny. To ask.

But instead of asking, Emile freshens Stu's drink, then Daphne's, then his own. He admires Stu's new casting rod and they make vague fishing plans. He inspects Daphne's shortwave radio, and they all listen on the patio intently to a German broadcast, accompanied by Stu's halting translation. That is what makes Emile and Penny's father ostensibly close: the military. Emile has a better grasp of German from his college classes but defers to Stu's age and rank and stories of revelry in Amsterdam. Emile has been, understandably, reluctant to discuss his brief stint in Mannheim at age nineteen, not there six months before he married his first real girlfriend. She wasn't even a German girl but an army brat, the daughter of the chaplain. Her face now a blur but full then, as broad and anguished as the moon; she delivered stillborn the end of an era. Penny has told her parents of this, no doubt, but he offers it up to them anyway in short form: *I don't know if Penny ever told you about my first marriage I was very young just trying to do right by her the baby died it seemed there was no more reason to be married shipped back to the States had a whole other life. Met your daughter.* There he places the emphasis.

An impromptu afternoon wine tasting was where Emile met Penny; where Emile met anyone, for that matter. If enough people toured the winery, then lingered in the gift shop, Emile was prone to start opening bottles. It boosted sales, and people left jovially, with high color on their cheeks. That fit Emile just right, he felt, to be a giver of good cheer. Last year was a pivotal time for the winery. They were just evolving past the sweet Catawbas and Concords into Zinfandels and Merlots. Still a little brackish, the new batches, but not without promise.

Penny had come only to make a purchase, but Emile convinced her to join the others who had congregated for the tour. She was the snide, strange, messy sort of pretty he liked. "It will give you a good story to tell," he tempted, "when you serve this wine. You can tell them how it's made." She'd been all over town that day, making arrangements for an open house her company would be throwing to show off their new offices, or "digs," as she called them, with a mild smirk. She'd been assigned to coordinate the snacks, greasy meatballs and cheese chunks to skewer on toothpicks, and she thought it would be good to offer some local wines, both to pay homage to the community and to unclog the arteries of those who were reckless enough to eat the snacks. "I'm almost certain we'd be liable," she quipped. Emile got the feeling she was always quipping and that it wearied her.

After the fifth or so sampling, most of the others were leaving, bottles under their arms. Again at Emile's prompting, Penny stayed on, still sipping, and eating crackers, "to line my stomach," she said. "I didn't have lunch today. Inspecting all those meatballs . . ." She scrunched her face. Emile asked what her job was, and she explained that her title was Administrative Assistant, "sort of a catchall name for one who does everything nobody else wants or is able to do." On a typical day, her duties might range from reconfiguring the network to taking out the garbage. "Secretary" denoted a finite set of duties, she claimed. She was, by now, wishing she were "only a secretary." But one problem: She was a horrible typist! Being extremely flexible had helped to conceal that fact.

Emile felt he was getting glimpses into a strange and mysterious world. He'd held many jobs but thus far had managed to avoid being sealed inside an office. The business types did visit the winery frequently enough, but he rarely got to know them past brief attempts at one-upmanship over tasting terms. Wine was a business-type person's show-off hobby, Emile believed. But this one, in her ill-fitting blazer, knew little about wine. She tipped back each thimbleful, sweet or dry, with equal enthusiasm. It had been a while—long enough, he reasoned—since he'd connected with a woman, and she would do, she would certainly do. He opened for them what would be a very good bottle of Cabernet Sauvignon, given one more year. Now, a year later, he thinks of that wine, how it would have grown subtly richer and many-layered, how even Penny might appreciate it now.

It was too late in the afternoon, luckily, for Penny to have to return to work. She looked at her watch and announced, "Quitting time," then ceased her funny odd talk of her office and encouraged Emile to tell her about himself. He felt, palpably, that the modes had shifted. He became aware of her youth then; the few worried, cynical lines in her face that had aged her were relaxing smooth. Penny was doing a little math of her own as she listened to him, gauging age from all the places he'd lived, all the jobs. At her age, which Emile guessed to be early twenties, he had been just newly cured of his innocence, and he supposed some of that still clung to him, as nothing more terrible had happened. He knew he'd managed to hold the pallor, the outlines, of youth. And within himself he perceived only the merest slackening, a fatigue that was creeping in earlier in his bike rides.

They decided Penny should drive Emile home, ostensibly to get a better view of the grounds—an extension of the tour "for special customers only," he joked. Emile wedged his bicycle into the back of her car and loaded a case of assorted wines into the trunk. It was getting closer to harvest, and the grapevines edging the parking lot were vibrant and beaded with purple. The yield was pretty but insubstantial, he explained to Penny as they drove past. They brought in the bulk of their grapes from California. It would be years yet before the winery was fully self-sufficient again. It was experiencing a rebirth after Prohibition days, when the fields had been razed and the cellars used to cultivate mushrooms. Emile honored bearing witness to its slow, sure rebuilding. The wine would be good, was already drinkable.

Emile's house was more of a hut really, set forlornly at the edge of an abandoned field. They seemed to be miles from town but were barely out of the winery's backyard. The vineyards had at one time been vast, extending out to these now wide and weedy spaces. Penny's little car lurched up the sparsely graveled driveway, and she yanked the emergency brake up. The motor still running, she turned to him quizzically: What now?

"Do you like cats?" Emile asked her. Penny nodded. "You have to meet the animals," Emile urged. "They love women; haven't seen one in months." He wasn't sure if this sounded good or bad, but Penny went inside, sat on his sofa, and gathered them to her. They engulfed her almost at once, the three of them, nudging and purring, swatting jealously at each other. Emile nodded approvingly, then excused himself to quickly inspect the rest of his house. He shoved clothes under the bed, sniffed around for litter box stench, and went to the kitchen for food. After some foraging, he returned to the den with crackers, olives, and cheese, and was surprised to find her sleeping, the cats sprawled out along the length of her. He knelt by the sofa and stroked her shoulder tentatively, but her sleep was so deep and trusting he didn't disturb her again that night.

Their beginnings were pure, he likes to tell people.

Yes, Penny has mentioned he was married before. Daphne rests her hand lightly at Emile's elbow. Stu directs his gaze benevolently into the blue-orange dusk. Emile appreciates the light touch of their response. He's relieved even though he has rarely met anyone who was *not* understanding about his first marriage. Though Penny can be hard and act as if she has lost more—and perhaps that is much of the attraction, Emile thinks behind the gin, stirring it with his index finger, swirling it in the glass. He shifts in his folding chair, and the cane fibers split and bite the backs of his thighs. Where might he be instead of on this parents' patio, balking at his own intentions? He likes Penny's parents, loves Penny, but right now he has lost sight of what seemed like the best idea—get the money down—only days earlier, when he was struck resolutely with the notion of ownership.

Yesterday, today even, *ownership* has been ringing in his head as he considers how he has come so thoroughly to know his remote and funky rental house, from its flaky plaster walls through to its warped aluminum siding, from its lightly shedding roof down to its concrete pad. It is at best a modest property, cheap and livable. It holds no secrets from him, and he wants to possess it. Proportionally, he knows it is a small request to make of Penny's parents. They don't appear to have the retirees' frugality he sees in his own parents, but they have made wise investments; he knows they have "set aside" a good bit for their daughter. And they are, without question, delighted with Emile.

Still, he hesitates; there remains that leftover splinter of shame his own parents have embedded in him, which prickles when he is about to appall them. And they would be appalled that he did not consult them first in order that they might disapprove, then offer him a loan with blood and nerves and guilt interest. Another disappointment, and that he has thus far failed to mantle them with grandchildren. But he wants that goddamn house, and he will ask at the end of this drink or the next.

If he ever got quite this way over Penny, Emile suspects he could grovel to her parents—or even his—without reluctance, but he doesn't want to "own" Penny, flaws and all. Inhabit Penny? This he isn't convinced he could do, or try, the way she inhabits him. Her puzzling remarks are always reverberating. "An apple wouldn't rot in here," she once said of his house. What did she mean? Or what he has come to know of as her behavior modificational silences. If the topic shifts too suddenly or without her approval, she will sometimes just stop talking, won't even respond to questions. But he has grown accustomed to all her "caprices," as he calls them. She is pretty in an unfinished, haphazard way. She is smart. She doesn't seem so young but is—a good combination. He is addicted to her light, sensual gestures—the way her tongue flickers across his eyelids, for example, or the brief pleasurable flare of her nostrils when he enters her. The way her pinkie traces the rim of her teacup. Idle details, but vital to Emile, enriching. Women have a way of filling in his gaps, solidifying him. Penny is a live-in, but he isn't sure yet what else. It isn't that Emile absolutely wouldn't marry again, but so far none after that first has made it past the living together stage. And most have had potential.

So this commitment to a house he is somewhat sheepish to reveal, especially after his sudden inexplicable confession. Penny's parents will think he was just trying to soften them up, and isn't he? Or is he just saying anything to postpone the blank, embarrassed expressions people get when they are asked for money? In a way, Emile rationalizes, it's like a credit check. He is inviting them to look into his history. They may ask questions if they wish, reevaluate his character. He is fairly certain he would welcome this, respect their judgment. As long as it is vindicating.

For the duration of her wait in traffic, Penny seethes quietly against Emile. Over the weekend, he said to her quite matter-of-factly, "*I will buy the house and you can live here as part owner if you wish,*" but at the time she heard only *you . . . live . . . here (with me)*, the invitation and the promise in it, and she hung on him like rags, fluttering: *let me think let me think yes.* Yes. But now, embittered by her day Penny feels excitement give way to brooding. Suddenly she's believing he wants an advantage and he thinks this new arrangement will give it to him. Her office dress is too snug and spangled with cheery polka dots, and this adds to her fury. She cannot get over thinking work is keeping her from something important, and the time it exacts is blood from her veins. Yet she will appear before her parents in the exact manner they wish to see her, their career girl vision, with a man of whom they utterly approve, despite the age difference. She hadn't realized until he spoke of Vietnam and Watergate with some authority, events that were no more than cultural memories for Penny. Yet they act as if his being sixteen years older is somehow to accommodate them. How thoughtful of Penny to finally choose not only a nice man but one her parents could better *relate* to!

Penny considers bursting in and cursing them all soundly, then spearing some choice meat from the grill to take back to the apartment she still occupies alone, at least through the end of next month, when the lease runs out. She'll crouch by the sofa and eat it with her hands, all the lights off and some wildlife documentary glimmering from her TV set, Penny with the leopards or cheetahs tearing off primal chunks with their teeth.

This is the traffic thinking and the long day, muses Penny, and putting two and two together and getting three: my mother, my father, and Emile. Penny called home to check her answering machine messages before leaving work and heard Emile say, "Hey, love. I'm going ahead to your folks, so I'll meet you there." That he would seek out their company should please her, she knows, but instead it alarms and irritates her, thoughts of where their conversation might flow unchecked: *Before Penny (Judith) could barely walk, she was eating right out of the dog bowl. . . . When Penny went to get her driver's license, she backed into a telephone pole.* Penny fully expects to find the three huddled over photo albums: *Oh, here she is all dressed up for her junior prom, so pretty. (When she wasn't home by one, we called the police.)* In one album, they have actually left the few pages past her high school years blank, before resuming with photos of Penny moving into her apartment, standing by her just purchased car, recent shots of her and Emile at the dinner table. *Penny had a few, well, problems in college. We don't have so many pictures from then.*

Those empty pages hold invisible images, her parents' secret, terrified suspicions of what Penny did in college. It was a place she entered completely unequipped for freedom. She found only brief sanctuary in the rituals of her sorority, their careful preparations, the streamlining of dress: formal days, casual days. Regimen, Penny believed for a short time, would save her. Sisterhood was a cloak of safety she could wear. The girls would bicker and meddle and hug each other to graduation. But Penny was drawn to the ones with cynical lines around their eyes, unkempt for sorority types: the hair not quite right, the dissident makeup—mouths too red or not enough, mascara caked or absent. They stayed slender and terse with cocaine, and when that was unavailable, methamphetamines.

Penny didn't care for the surgical numbness cocaine brought; she felt she was being prepped for a root canal. But meth blasted her sinuses, an honest, caustic burn. Meth crackled beneath the surface of her skin; everything tingled like after a sneeze, but for hours. It was cheap and easy to get; she once met a guy who made it in his bathtub. On meth, Penny lost the seam between day and night. It was worth the twitchy sleep that she fell into much, much later. Light or dark, she was a

surging forward motion—but at night there were the parties.
Penny loved the boys who swaggered around there, pungent
with aftershave and beery lust. She loved to peel back denim
or broadcloth to skin; she loved their skin. When they touched
her, she wouldn't stop; why should she stop? Pleasure was in
drawing pleasure out of the other; pleasure was in being the
culprit. It seemed impossible that there could be any other
kind. The sensation was of losing the familiar outlines of herself, warping, extending, merging. Her classes, introductory,
confirmed it, defined her. She was the sinuous foot of a mollusk.
She amassed territory like a ruthless general, infinite as a vari-
able. A slow swirl in a crucible, her change was chemical, mo-
lecular, her shifts were plate tectonic. Mortified, the sisters fell
away from her—heavy scales she shed relieved. Then she got
pregnant, and again. Stoic, out of charter obligation, two girls
escorted her to the clinic. There she was cold-blooded, verte-
brate, her eggs abandoned in the sand.

Someone called her parents, finally. Penny went away
with them easily; it was all of a piece anymore, to be in college
or not. She had missed the small things, like slender disks of cu-
cumber in her mother's salads. She would fish them out and
drape them, cooling, over her eyelids. Her mother exclaiming
in irritation, mild and forgiving. Her father puttering, puttering, tools appending his waist. Careful days, couched in normalcy. After months of apologia, she found her open spaces
again, but quietly. If she holds down a job, is fairly conscientious
about her grooming, does not drink or drug to excess, displays
a trademark wit, maintains a polite correspondence with some
of her ex-sorority sisters, is courted by an earnest man yet stays

radiantly barren out of wedlock, nobody will call for her parents again.

And Emile? He is good for Penny, she feels. Next to his sheer force of years, her troubles seem like small change. Penny has always loved the pathos of Emile's history and the way he told it. He knelt by his sofa after that first night—she'd fallen asleep on it, weary from the wine and narcotic talk, knowing this had been a charming thing to do. He offered her sips of orange juice and murmured his life to her. He promised a core of sadness she could tap into, nearly a whole life ahead of hers.

Penny is sure Emile would have made a nice father, would have taken to it easily. He is a good sport about things. Penny imagines the baby at times as a sort of wispy, ephemeral cherub hovering around Emile's shoulders. That is the sort of ghost that would linger, she thinks, a baby, although perhaps it is more likely to tail the mother. She thinks the mother is remarried, though, and has had another child, which would displace the ghost. Though Penny had the two abortions, there were never any ghosts. She firmly believes that sort of thing is reserved for fully formed babies. What would her ghosts be? Cell clusters, zygotes—more like fish floating in the ether. Penny cannot project her accidents into the world. Thinking of the alternative, she sees only herself, ragged and lunatic, flaccid breasts drooling milk into the ground.

When Penny warns Emile that she may be crazy, he says only *You are, you are*, and shrugs.

· · ·

A minivan drifts casually into her lane and Penny swerves, thrusting the heel of her hand into the horn. Its plaintive bleat seems to spurt from her own lungs, and the minivan jerks abruptly back into its own lane. If she hates anyone, it's this minivan driver playing it so fast and loose with all their lives. The thing Penny fears worst is being killed from someone's stupidity or negligence. She will cook canned green beans for twenty minutes to avoid such a fate. The fact that some random, careless action could take her out reminds her she is angry.

But again, she knows it is the long day and she's off kilter. Penny has been taking medication to balance out her moods; she was, until recently, a believer in the mild-dosage approach to unbridled angst or bottoming out. But it has been stinging her to urinate lately, and the summer brought with it one protracted yeast infection. The more she read about chemical levels in the body, the more convinced she became that the drug is at fault; it has thrown her off. There has been an illicit thrill to reducing the dose on her own *recognizance*, so to speak. She's receiving near-forgotten surges of her former normalcy, that hyperawareness, an absorption that at times consumed her. All day she has been transfixed by the glistening dots of flesh in the corners of people's eyes. As if veiled, their talk sifted through to her, yet she responded, she's fairly certain, in all the appropriate manners. And now she's confident of her command over this vehicle; it's a flesh knowledge, born of necessity, to carry her safely to her appointed destination.

A liturgy of familiars: third exit ramp, left, left, right, the flower-garlanded chicken painted on her parents' mailbox, the double bump over the seam between tar road and concrete driveway. Cheery brick ranch, all-season wreath on the open door; Penny breezes through pastel shag and country crafts and has a mild amused pang over the latest, a rough-hewn kitchen bin marked *taters n' onions*. Through the kitchen to the patio. Gazing at her three, whose faces tilt up to her in welcome, Penny basks in how age softens all their edges, flab puddling benign in the crooks of arms. Reconfigured, they would encircle her.

Penny's arrival imminent, Emile bolsters himself and asks Penny's parents for the money. To help buy his house, he explains. To have something outright. Heat begins seeping red through his cheeks, but he fights it—better to be pale and serious, he figures.

There are questions. Estimates? Long-term potential? Acreage? Square footage? Wiring? Plumbing? They don't ask, mercifully, why he is approaching them with his request, nor do they ask about his "intentions" toward their daughter. But he tells them, anyway, the extent of what he knows about that: "Penny's going to live there with me and split the payments." Stu shifts uneasily in his seat and begins rolling his new casting rod between his palms.

"*Live* there," echoes Daphne. "What *as*?" There is alarm in her voice, but muted. Emile recognizes her voice as a gravelly version of Penny's; the inflections are almost identical. Daphne is the shape into which Penny will metamorphose: the rounded shoulders will slope in increments, the hands will spot and grow corded, odd hairs and spidery red veins will sprout, flesh will pull into white striations. Emile has made love to women who would now be Daphne's age, and he wonders if that possibility has ever occurred to her or Stu.

Or to Penny, who has sliced through the house and halted at the screen door, where she now regards them, nose denting the mesh.

"Hey, Jude," Emile calls to her.

"There's the career girl, Judith Boyd," sings Daphne.

"Judy," says Stu. Then, backtracking, "Penny."

Penny's eyes glint in recognition of Stu. "That's right," she affirms, but she doesn't open the door. "Go ahead with your conversation," she says. "I just need a few minutes."

"I'll get you a drink," offers Stu, but Penny presses her palm into the webbing: Stop. Soon she will slide open the door and join them on the patio, but for now she is enjoying the thin membrane of screen between them.

The parents each look meaningfully at Emile. Somehow they understand he has not consulted Penny about coming to them for a loan. They are protecting him—protecting her, maybe. Why? "It's all right," says Emile. He is saying it to all of them. He is looking at Penny. Her face is stricken blank; she needs those few minutes like air.

"You come on out here with us," he coaxes anyway, and she does, suddenly all right.

Penny likes to stand by the grill with her father and paint the ribs with Worcestershire sauce, so she does. Daphne likes to scrutinize Penny's work hair, clothes, and waistline, murmuring compliments, so she does. Stu likes to prong the meat and flip it and flip it and poke the coals that are there just for show, so he does. Emile likes to regard them all warmly, saying little or nothing, just watching the parents flank the daughter, familial shapes that soothe. But he doesn't. He outlines his plans again, this time for Penny's benefit. She whirls around, her basting brush dripping juice, and exclaims, "I have it. I have five thousand dollars."

"That's for your school," reminds Daphne. "For when you go back."

"I won't go back," says Penny. "Believe it."

Stu piles the meat on a plate and swings the grill lid shut with a clang. Penny is already gnawing a rib bone on her way to the table. She never mentions the cut-glass pitcher, and there aren't enough leftovers to carry back, so they leave empty-handed. Stu and Daphne are grim with concern but embrace Penny at the door. Daphne kisses Emile on the cheek. Stu grasps his hand.

"Take care," they admonish the couple. "Take care."

"Follow you home?" Penny suggests to Emile in the driveway, and he agrees: "My house is yours."

It is a weeknight, which Emile knows is likely to mean sleep only. Penny is sullen about the early mornings and hoards her rest. Still, there is the possibility of gentle ambush. She is wearily acquiescent, and if he were to sling himself lazily atop her in the dark, after her breathing has changed, it would be all right. She is lax about precautions, though, and this, with her limp body weighted from sleep, edges her vulnerability, lends him an uneasy power. He knows she won't stop him for the bathroom trip; she is thick with trust, half dreaming. It is not his intention, outright, to impregnate her, but at the times that he can have her this way—her womb not jelled with toxins to resist him—he is struck with a fatalistic optimism.

Penny is sleeping on her side, curled, her back to Emile. The cats nicker and growl, circling the bed. One by one they leap up to absorb her warmth, and Emile gently scoops each in turn back onto the floor. He strokes Penny's side, rests his hand under the warm jut of her hip. Awake, Penny would squeeze her excess flesh he strokes between thumb and forefinger, as if it were evidence. She seems to want him to agree she is fat beyond redemption, but to Emile she is only natural, fleshy. "You're not a triathlete," he tells her. "You're not a gangly preadolescent. You're not anorexic. So what?" "I want to be angular," she laments, "but I'm round." He has told her how he hates angular women: the bladed cheekbones, the famine-dry expanse of the pelvis, the prehensile spine tail extending to the buttocks. He prefers softness, he has told her, and, beneath that, solidity—and of course it is an insult. It is insulting to say I love what you are to these women with impossible ideals; they want to believe it is for you they are suffering. Nearly two decades of being the Boyfriend has convinced Emile of this, but he remains determined, nonetheless, to stand his ground. Someone will accept this with grace. Penny could learn to yet. She is still young. He strokes her hip intently, and she stirs.

The cats have claimed Penny as their own; in her absence, they sleep in the recess her body leaves in the mattress; they search for her everywhere. She senses their gentle stalking; upon striking, they will feast in the warmth of her belly. In her sleep self she is already moving in, and the house turns out its pockets to her, shelves gap to hold her things, hooks for cups and coats beckon. She is projecting her posters onto the walls, wedging her bureau between his nightstand and the closet. Her furniture is balsa wood, light as air; just a nudge, and momentum will set them right. Leaned in, warm, it seems the very house is caressing her, but it is Emile, heavy as a house, a furnace glowing her awake. No, it is the other way around: she is the dwelling, deep, rooted underground, and he is a mole, snuffling, scrabbling to unearth her; his burglar claws have broken all her seals, and he seeps in like rain. Then she is awake and he is solid flesh and she is moving beneath him, pushing, rocking, holding on, while they gather the force and momentum to propel themselves into another world.

FIGHT
OR
FLIGHT

———

Bernadette and I have gotten so we play "There's the Rapist," where we point out certain skanky-looking guys wandering around our neighborhood.

"There he is," one of us says, not loudly, but not whispering either.

"That's him all right," says the other. "Just look at those eyes. What do you think he's got in that knapsack?"

"Oh, gloves, rope, duct tape. Tools of the trade."

"Gun or knife?"

"Hmm . . . I'd say gun, but not loaded. He just jams it into the small of your back for emphasis. This one's not a cutter."

"I disagree. Because why else those boots if not to slide a knife down?"

"Very astute. They don't look much good for running."

And so forth. We size him up from a fair distance, and it's daylight, so I feel pretty brave. Bernadette has kicked in the door to her boyfriend's apartment more than once, and she knows a karate move where you slam the heel of your hand into a guy's nose so it will shove his septum right up into his brain. Me, I've got my little pink canister of pepper spray on a key chain. Just flip the nozzle and press, and you send a searing stream of irritant into the eyes of your would-be attacker. But it's nontoxic, and I like that.

"You have to have a thing like that in your hand and ready, if it's going to be any use," says Bernadette, and I know that, but we're on a friendly jog in broad daylight. I don't want to scare the neighborhood kids or freak people out. I keep it tucked in the waistband of my sweatpants, and it's no bigger than a lipstick. I could grab it in an instant, even if it has adhered to my soft, sweating stomach.

"We need to get out more," I tell Bernadette, "or I'm going to lose it in the folds of my skin."

"You just carry that thing for psychological reasons, but it's not really going to help you. You have a false sense of security." Bernadette quickens the pace.

Bernadette mocks me with her rude good health, her pert, insolent ponytail. I jounce and sweat along beside her, my skin festering under Lycra and fleece. My breasts ache with the jostling, but I cannot bring myself to do as she advises, which is to cup each wayward dug firmly in the palms and press them stationary against the chest to prevent "tissue damage." I envision instead a system of pulleys, a gravity-defying harness, or, better, a chest as sleek and muscled as a young boy's. Her own breasts bob cheerily.

"Go ahead," I finally manage between ragged gasps. "I'm going to walk." I've got to walk, really, or fall down. I do better supine, splayed across a sofa, plucking yogurt raisins from a decorative tin. I take on the rumpled, sexy look of lavish indolence. A body at rest tends to want to stay at rest. As her ponytail flounces away, my walk loses its emphasis, takes on the lackadaisical nature of a stroll. When she rounds the block back to me, I will pick it up again, pumping the arms mightily. But not until my calves stop convulsing and the staccato of my pulse has tapered down a bit.

Alone, I know you should walk briskly and with confidence, but ready to run or scream before the danger is upon you, and not be embarrassed it might be a false alarm. Women are more concerned about being embarrassed than about being harmed, it seems! Not Bernadette. Once she was coming out of the Value Barn with an armload of groceries, and this guy starts to ask her directions. She hollered *No!* loud enough for people to turn around, and he backed right off. "Jeez, lady!" he exhorted, palms turned out.

"But, Bernadette," I said when she told me. "You don't know that he meant you any harm."

"Doesn't matter," she said. "I have the right." And I know she's being smart, but what if some nice-looking guy in a tailored suit—cuff links and the whole bit—comes up to you? Just spit in his face, I guess, because he could certainly be one. How are you supposed to meet anybody? And how would you know, even one, two, five dates, six months, two years down the road, what they are capable of? Until it happens.

"They're all potentials," Bernadette says, but she also says, "Go with your instincts," and my instinct might be to just give the guy directions, even after all this practice scoping out the neighborhood. I'm just not getting any better sense of who's regular and who's rapist. I simply point at any scuzzy guy walking down the sidewalk, and Bernadette agrees. I get a real chill, though, when she points them out, like she knows better than me. I only know some things about them; they aren't necessarily scuzzy, for example. And they don't pick out the littlest or weakest-looking ones; they pick out the ones who look uncertain, easy to intimidate. That would be me now, and weak besides. Though what I want is to look strong, to be strong.

Living alone does something to you that way. The first few weeks on my own were uneasy at best. It has never gotten completely dark in my little apartment; the streetlight coaxes dim outlines of things. My clothes flung over a chair would take the shape of a man, huddled and pensive. I'd peer at them until the details sharpened to a sleeve or the cup of a bra. It took time to assimilate the night sounds. No soft scratch or creak could go unidentified. Five times a night I'd get up to test the door, twisting and tugging the knob to make sure it wouldn't give. It took a lot for me not to try patching things up with Calvin just to end those anxious nights. Pride, I figured out it was.

Now, alone is not so bad. I can smear my hands with Vaseline and wear rubber gloves to bed, or glob zit cream on a bump. My legs get prickly, I eat a can of beets for supper; who's the wiser? I am learning to enjoy this privacy. Sometimes I do not even lunge across the room to answer the phone. I just let it ring. If I am reading or listening to music, the time has become valuable to me. It used to be stasis, that hour or two between my return home from work and Calvin's. I was poised in a chair, magazine open, prop wineglass between my fingers, just filler until he came home and I could come alive again. I was the woods in that riddle where no felled tree would sound without a listener.

Springing up the sidewalk toward me are three boys ranging from pre- to mid-adolescence. The shortest one bounces a soccer ball, while a bigger boy brings up the rear, stomping on the ball-bouncer's heels. The tallest, an aloof overseer in a hooded sweatshirt and shorts that flap around his bony knees, flicks his cigarette away at the sight of me. Because of me? It doesn't seem so; the slack mouth and averted eyes appear indifferent. His cigarette glances off one of the concrete lions curled sleepily at the driveway of the Dupree house, that beveled-glass-and-cupola pseudo mansion, its soft green lawn pungent with roses. Most of the rest of us living in this aging neighborhood rent apartments in saggy, vinyl-sided houses; the yards that will never belong to us are thick and brambled with wayward shrubs and cheap perennials. I admire the gesture of contempt—I, too, despise the show-offs.

I practice my confident body language on these boys; I know their mothers. I stick to the sidewalk, straighten my spine, and stride resolutely, making brief, noncommittal eye contact with each of them—better that than to look away. I hold the sidewalk. They give way, scattering to each side of me, into the grass, into the street, allowing me the straight path through.

"There goes your wife," one says, just as I've passed, and they all snicker.

I knew they could not just let me pass without tossing something out. Boys slightly older would not even have conceded the sidewalk. The world belongs to these boys, young and bursting with innocent violence. The same fists that casually pummel desks and countertops and walls gather force, momentum, and soon they are arcing into flesh. I thought I was safe with Calvin, had in fact been choosing safety, but soon enough I kissed his rough, implacable knuckles, felt the wet heft of bone split my weak cushion of lips to meet bone. No one was more shocked than he was. I, at least, had seen it coming.

At the mile-and-a-half marker (the Helbrandts' concrete goose dressed in a bonnet and apron), I start to play our game alone. The rapist on the corner, unshaven but just shy of scummy, nudges the bill of his cap at me. He's got this mushy flop-eared hush-puppy dog on a leash—just a decoy, I think, a trick to make me stop and coo, disarmed. Stroking the silky head and lost in the brown eyes of this dog, I will be vulnerable to attack. I decide, recklessly, to play along. I have, after all, a protective device.

"What a sweet puppy!" I exclaim, and stop to give it a friendly pat. My other hand pats at my waist for the pepper spray, but I realize too late that it has dropped down into my panties, the old, stretched-out ones I wear for exercise, so the elastic has given out. Like a tiny erection, the slender metal cylinder juts from my crotch.

Our eyes meet. The rapist grins.

"Beautiful day," he says.

"Yes indeed," I say.

"Out for a walk?" he asks.

"Just getting some fresh air," I say evasively. I'm not about to admit that, well, it began as a jog but I'm too worn out, too weak.

"Well, it's a good day for it."

"Yes. Beautiful day." I stroke the dog fiercely. "Good girl. Nice girl." The dog collapses in ecstasy, rolling onto her back. We are running out of innocent conversation, and soon, I fear, I will have to plunge a hand down the front of my sweatpants to retrieve the pepper spray. I am very reluctant to do so, though his eyes glitter menacingly, and I realize I am of those women whose instinct is first and foremost to avoid embarrassment. How methodically I leaned into the steering wheel of my car not so many months ago, gauging the height, guessing at the im-pact necessary to explain my swollen mouth.

Could I outrun him? It's doubtful—I'm still winded. I tug the drawstring of my pants, still nodding, still smiling. Nice puppy.

A hand grasps my shoulder, and I flinch in terror. But it is only Bernadette, who has rounded the block back to me. Beau-tiful, bursting-with-brute-strength Bernadette. She will never allow any harm to come to me!

Still jogging in place, she nods curtly to the rapist and his dog bait. "Come on, lazy. You've got to keep your heart rate up, or it's no good," Bernadette scolds, and strong-arms me down the sidewalk with her. Soon we are running, our arms still linked, shoes smacking the pavement in sync. When our distance has reduced the rapist to a speck, we criticize him.

"So obvious!"

"Thoroughly amateur."

"My kid brother could pull off a better one than that!"

Laughing, gulping the good air, we pick up our pace.

TERMS OF
THE LEASE

The students descend from mysterious, rent-free summers
with neotribal swirls or Greek letters tattooed on shoulders and ankles. Tans waning, they're already grappling with
the issues; they're writing papers on date rape, the injustices
dealt to Native Americans, hemp legalization. By Thursday of
week one, they are ready to get down to some serious partying.
And because of their tattoos, their ritualistic hairstyles, I figure
they mean business. I am right. Their howls prickle the hair
along my neck; their feet, shod for hiking or combat, stomp
down the halls of my apartment building; the walls hum and
fissure with their music; the vents sift their frantic coupling
sounds in the night. I am the traditional one here, stolid and
prim in my homemade jumpers, mired in the back-to-school
celibacy of the newly divorced. I work for a living, drive a mid-
size car, own a first-generation sofa. When the summer ends

and my blissfully hollow building is alive again with chittering, glass breaking, and the blood-heavy thrum of bass, I feel most especially like a die-cut adult.

I say *my* building, but I only manage it, and perhaps manage is too strong a word after August. *Maintain* seems more to the point, though I call on Maintenance for anything more than spackle or a plunger can right. I call on the police to restore order, or Morty, the owner, whose cancer-raspy pleas for compliance shame even the most seasoned of partyers and rent dodgers. *Accept* is what I mostly do until the end of May, when the nine-month leases have run their course. Then I *retain*: security deposits mostly, but sometimes furniture, clothing, housewares left behind. Next, I *remove*: the odor of urine or vomit, the traces of covert pets, hair- and shit-festooned carpets that the steam cleaner strips down to burlap. In my former incarnation, as prideful predivorcée, I said I would not be somebody's kitchen slave, but summer comes, my head enters fifty ovens, and, filing out the glops of carbon, I feel the little death each time. Too bad the ovens are electric, too bad they are only enameled old gold or avocado, too bad nobody ever bakes anything more ambitious in them than frozen pizza or brownies from mix.

Did I mention I sleep alone in a bed littered with books? I roll over and pretend the corners poking me are the sharp hips and elbows of my lover, abysmally thin and exhausted by desire. I'm not fooled, of course, by my own petty fantasy; I have a 4.0 average in spite of the constant buzz of distraction that surrounds me. I like to think of my corner two-bedroom unit in building A as the eye of the storm. The spare bedroom is my study, though it holds three twin beds, extras in case the tenants need to crowd in another roommate. I am supposed to discourage this, but want very much to be rid of the beds. It is ridiculous to have so many beds when I sleep alone, plus they beckon when I am at my desk, an island in the sea of mattresses. I generally keel right over from my desk chair onto one of these beds and wake up with my hair all mashed and my bra digging into my ribs. My classes are my only truly satisfying source of intensity and exhaustion these days. I let them ravish me.

My study overlooks a busy intersection and the campus beyond. Southfork Manor is a prime location because the students need only tear themselves out of bed about ten minutes before class and they can still work in a shower without being too late. Despite this rent-enhancing convenience, they all drive cars, it seems. The lot clears of tenants by nine, the commuters sneak in, and I chalk their tires for the tow truck. Then classes, lunch, classes, the library, perhaps, and home before dark. By then, the answering machine is pulsing a stacatto red dot, signaling clogged toilets, foul odors, misplaced keys, blown fuses, forbidden pet sightings. The tenants are a surly and vengeful lot, bent on wreaking eviction on enemy neighbors. Spackle and plunger within arm's reach, I return calls, placate, separate emergency from mild inconvenience, compile a list from most to least compelling household dramas.

Today I punch the message button and reports of the supernatural trickle in from all four floors, both buildings. Goo on the walls, blood from the faucet, ephemeral creatures flit-

ting from closet to closet. The pantry or john is a good ten de-
grees colder than the rest of the apartment. "I just had a feeling,
an indescribable feeling, come over me," reports 3A. "Could we
be built over an ancient burial ground?" Strictly Hollywood-
style phenomena. I suspect practical joking on a grand scale
and will not be moved. "Sounds like a vermin problem," I say as
mildly as I can to the tenants when I return their calls. "I'll send
Maintenance over."

Maintenance consists of Eddie, a retired drywaller, and
his son Chas, who Eddie says is slow. They supposedly live
somewhere in building B, but I have only ever found them in
the basement workshop, which is equipped with a TV, twin re-
cliners, and a hot plate. I suspect they are subletting their own
apartment, but what can be done?

"Afternoon, Mrs. Finkle," says Eddie. He and Chas call me
Mrs. Finkle because I am a matronly thirty-two amid lithesome
twentysomethings. "Ready for another go at it?" By this he
means school, the students, another headlong plunge toward
winter. These final days of August are what Eddie calls
"whiskey weather," not so much from the heat as from the sudden influx of tenants scrabbling overhead in demand of his ser-
vices. Eddie wears long underwear in the cool of the basement
evenings, and flip-flops. His toenails are as thick and yellow as
the layers of paste wax in the corridors. He fishes around in a
Styrofoam cooler for an ice cube, which he plunks unabashedly
into his whiskey glass.

"Eddie, it seems that the building is haunted," I say with
great weariness and disgust. The students are haunting *me*. I
think of the paper waiting for me back at my desk. The topic:

the date rape of the Native Americans by hemp-wielding militiamen who lured them out of the Black Hills with the promise of dinner and a matinee. The superior hemp rope product may have enabled them to bind wrists and ankles tight, but this is purely conjecture, a working thesis. I know I am addled.

Eddie knows it, too, and sloshes some of his whiskey into a cup for me. "Not my area of expertise, Mrs. Finkle," he admits.

"No, no," I tell him. "I just need you to tramp through some of the apartments with me and see if any real damage has been done." I want him to hem and haw with me and make it plain to these people that we are not amused by their chicanery. I want him to pencil estimates onto his clipboard pad while I mutter on about security deposits. In short, I need a lackey, or a henchman.

"Chas!" Eddie barks. Chas appears from behind the furnace, face smeared with jam. Chas is thirty-six, and though he is admittedly odd, I don't agree with Eddie's diagnosis of "slow," unless by that he means contemplative. I've looked behind that furnace, and there are about a thousand paperbacks on a wide range of subjects. Chas thumbs his forehead at me in a hat-tipping gesture, only he wears no hat.

"Chas, go with Mrs. Finkle and tell her what you know." Eddie turns to me. "He's got a sort of antenna for these things. He can tell you if it's a real problem."

"I know it's not a real problem," I say. "I know it isn't," but repeating it reveals my growing unease. What if the reports are exaggerations but not an all-out hoax? With a chill, I recall that Southfork Manor was built on the site of a disco that burned to the ground in 1976.

The calls are clearly hoaxes, Chas indicates after running his hands along the walls of the apartments we inspect. The tenants slink about, smirk and complain. Even their TVs whine, even their furniture splays helplessly across the floor. Their dresser drawers loll open in hangdog pouts, clothes drooling out the corners. Their living spaces are dulled of extraneous psychic activity, I infer from Chas's shrugs. He does sense some halos of energy around the beds, but these belong wholly to the tenants, he assures me.

I ask Chas to check my apartment, hoping he will target it as the source of the energetic disturbance. I want him to slide his hands across my wood-grain veneers and pronounce, "This desk is white hot."

But he only pauses in my hallway, expression blank, registering nothing. I thank him and return to my apartment alone—nothing new.

Another message winks from my machine. There's a coven meeting in 6B, claims the anonymous caller. I use my master key, don't even knock, and end up crashing a cosmetics party. The girls are draped in fabric swatches and reek of musky gardenias. They are layering scents and learning their individual color "seasons." It's a kind of alchemy, this belief that the right tones of makeup, the perfect shade of scarf wreathing the neck will transform a woman. I ask with some trepidation, "Any occult activity going on here?" and they just laugh and tuck a burgundy cloth in my collar to appraise me. "You're an absolute winter," one proclaims, and they all agree, but I must protest. Winter! Those cooped-up months battling the furnace and installing storm windows drive me to distraction. I live for spring, when the old leases begin to wither up and blow away, and the new tenants tentatively nudge their way in. They approach me neatly groomed, politely seeking shelter, and I am always filled with hope.

Work
Ethics

~~~~

Irene can't be there—a trip, planned weeks ago—but Merritt
should make himself at home. No sense in a hotel, the money
just wasted, and he can water her plants and finish off the milk
and potato salad. The key's beneath a loose brick at the head of
the walkway; twist it hard to the right. The bolt is stubborn,
the key rasps in the lock, but a fierce turn, leaning in with the
shoulder, will pop it right open.

   This apartment is smaller, narrow and dark, but otherwise
much is the same—Merritt recognizes her cheap rattan furniture, the thready aqua towels, Teflon peeling off her skillets
like sunburned skin. Even her juxtapositions are familiar: a
shoe in the magazine rack, a black bra and a cored apple among
the jumble of glossy catalogs on the coffee table. Her clothes are
strewn in a trail leading to the bathroom, crumpled crisp-dried
panties and shriveled nylons draped over the shower rod. The
wicker hamper is swollen and leaning, bright cottons peeping

through the slats, the lid tilted like a jaunty cap. There is no discernable space not given over to Irene's things. How could there ever have been room for him here?

Merritt's job interview is somewhat of a fluke, and an excuse, probably, for him to come up when he suspects he's no longer really invited. But now that he's gotten it and driven all this way, he's going to see the interview through. The drive has exhausted him, knotted his neck and calves. He will be early to bed and up at six to chafe his beard, wash with her scented soap, and drink a pot of her good Kenya coffee. Irene would, if she were here, nod approval at the gray and subtly striped suit hanging in his garment bag, his confident red-flecked tie.

He had been counting on that, and her advice: "Don't risk a clammy handshake. Keep your handshake hand under your butt on the drive over. Don't eat any eggs; have just a croissant. Don't wear that belt." He had wanted her to thumb through his portfolio, pull out all the weak, snively drawings, and organize the others for maximum impact. If she were here, she would surely do all that. She wants him to do well, maybe still wants him here.

He's not to worry about the clothing heaped on her bed; she's always changing her mind and flinging things about when packing, always last-minute frantic. Just sweep it all to the floor, she said. Merritt holds a skirt up to his waist. It seems smaller than he remembers her—has she lost weight? Irene was solider, he thinks, not so much a wearer of skirts.

Clean linens and extra blankets in the closet. He peels the old ones from the mattress and bunches them in a corner. The clean sheets, the extras, look familiar: lavender roses with a few faded blots of stain. He snaps the fitted sheet neatly into place and flips the top sheet across.

Familiar pattern, familiar routine; he'd always been the one to make their bed, to fuss about her growing jumbled piles of things when they encroached on his areas. Back at his parents' house, it has been plenty easy to backslide. His parents maintain things so well that in a very short time Merritt has come to feel he no longer has to, or even should. His mother makes regular sweeps of his room for dirty clothes and dishes, while his father keeps the cars washed and waxed. Fried, gravy-coated meals are prepared with comforting regularity. Merritt likes to think he's been doing his part, helping to keep his parents occupied. He views their retirement as long empty stretches, marked only by the succession of little tasks. They do ask sometimes, tentatively, about his plans. No nagging, just curious.

In the corner of Irene's bedroom is her rickety desk, but it holds a sleeker, more expensive-looking computer than the one Merritt remembers. Her new printer is a formidable box that requires its own side table. He made her set up her "office space" in the kitchen when they lived together; he couldn't abide the eerie green glow of the computer screen in their bedroom at night. Irene exposed him needlessly to radiation, he accused, but what he meant was technology. As a wire editor, she culled news from the computer; she was hooked into sources world-wide, through the phone lines, she explained to him. She kept sitting him down in front of it to demonstrate, but he felt utterly detached. "You can even draw with this," she tempted. "I can get you the programs," but he didn't want to draw on it. It seemed like a way of making perfect circles and squares, things he wasn't interested in making.

The desk is, of course, littered with papers. A split-open datebook is ringed, starred, and highlighted throughout with Irene's special codes, cryptic abbreviations like LNCH-MTG and APPT W/MAX. She appears to be busier these days, Merritt ascertains, flipping through the datebook, though it's not clear what she's busy doing. Work things, he supposes; her transfer involved a promotion of sorts. How you get promoted from one city's paper to another's made no sense to Merritt until she explained that one giant corporation owns the papers. "Isn't it insidious?" she laughed, then told him she had a month to move.

He sits in her chair, which is also new—a springy swivel chair with some high-tech curves—and imagines her perched there smartly, looking for news worth printing. He is tired from the drive, and the chair hugs him gently, curving into his lower back. He grips the armrests and leans. The chair tilts back smoothly, obligingly, and he props his heels up on her desk. Among all Irene's things, it is easy to sink into reverie.

It floored Irene when he chose to move back in with his parents rather than follow her here. But it was *her* good job, on her coattails—what was there for him so far away? "You won't rely on me," she accused, "you're so proud. But you'll go back to your folks at twenty-eight. Where's your pride about that? You don't have anything to keep you here." And that made him mad, because by "anything," he knew she meant salary, position, all the bullshit he hated and had thought she hated too, though she was smart and had stuck through college. She'd seemed almost

scornful and apologetic about that when they were first together, like, what else was there for her to do?

"I get money just for going, so why not?" she would say.
"It's better than flipping burgers." She had stopped saying that
during Merritt's stint as a fry cook. She said "digging ditches"
instead. Some of Merritt's friends teased him, saying Irene was
slumming. That didn't bother him. He was proud of her. He'd
been to college too, for a while, but it just seemed pointless. For
him, he would emphasize to Irene. He didn't want to seem to
put her down, because probably it was the right thing for her.

Hell, at first whatever Irene wanted had been okay by
Merritt. For the longest time he couldn't get over how she
wanted him, his unbelievable luck at that. "You are so beautiful,"
he would tell her, over and over, incredulous, her hair spilling
through his hands. Sometimes there was nothing outside of
Irene, softened by wine and stroking his back, his hips, Irene
rocking above him, beneath him, her soft moans surrounding him.

"You could do graphics," she began to say more often, after
he'd moved in. "Hell, you *do* graphics; you just don't get paid
for it."

This grew tiresome. "Yeah, and you *could* get off my goddamn case." Before Irene's job became such a big deal, he hadn't
minded her suggestions. They were meant as encouragements,
he knew, but she was starting to push. He knew his father had
sort of meandered around—drinking and whoring, his mother
said—when he was Merritt's age, and getting married had
pretty much straightened him out. Merritt had thought it

might be okay to have something like that in Irene. But there were things about his father that could never be altered: his Navy tattoos, his refusal to wear a suit, his whiskey stashed in the garage. There was still that undercurrent of wildness. Somehow Irene was biting in too deep, wanting changes that Merritt feared would undermine him completely.

"I work," he said to her. "What does it matter? I pay my part of the bills. Why's it got to be something big?"

"You're not happy," she accused. "You're just hand-to-mouth. You live for five o'clock and weekends. You should enjoy your work. You should like what you have to spend so much of your time doing. I mean, you'll always have to work, right?" This became her advantage, Merritt thought, once she got the transfer. Merritt wasn't doing anything he couldn't drop at once, in her estimation, to tag along with her. He could pick up a crappy job anywhere, right? Irene never said that, not exactly, but it was hovering in all their new silences, her constant expression an expectant, irritated *Well?*

It came to seem that going with Irene would be an admission about his life Merritt was not willing to make. His father lent him the truck, and Merritt got his stuff out of their apartment in less than a day. So little was his, really, just his clothes, the drafting table, the stereo, and a chest of drawers, but they crowded his old room at home—he would have to sit on the bed to draw.

When he went back to their apartment, meaning to help Irene move her stuff too, he found she had already rented a van. She was just slinging things around in there, no caution, no order. Her face was red and smeared, angry. He rearranged, stacked, and padded her things as best he could. He wanted her to get there with as much intact as possible. It was all he could do by then, though of course he cried, and she did too. Decisions had been made, plans set in motion. The distance would be neither convenient nor surmountable.

So where are those pictures of them she was so adamant about taking before the move? Merritt imagines she has flung them in a drawer, burned them even, after that time she called and said come up for Thanksgiving.

"I can't," he told her. "I have to work."

"Then I'll come down," she offered eagerly. They still loved each other, was Irene's attitude then. Shouldn't they still see each other when they could?

"No. No, don't." It would have been more than Merritt could take just then. It would just have made things worse, like the longing that still sickened his stomach. He needed time yet for that to settle. But all he could say to her was *No, don't.*

Her tone changed after that. She switched from phone calls to letters on office stationery, sometimes typed. They dwindled in length and frequency. Merritt was figuring then that his life would stay pretty much the same until he got his own place. Then it would resume its pre-Irene state, which was generally carefree, except for a terminal horniness occasionally relieved by a girl who was not Irene. But Irene's life would become something he'd never know, as she formed a new circle of friends, earned more money, found a lover. Her letters only hinted at the changes. "Things are going well and I hope so for you also. Love, i," the "i" lowercase and dotted with a heart or flower, sickly cute and not like what he knew. A small slap, a reproach.

Still. "I'm thinking of relocating," he called to tell her after too many months spent in his tiny, wood-paneled room, sitting on the bed to draw, drawing a lot. He still feels lethargy from all the fried chicken and cream soups; his mother has begun buying his shoes again. "There's a job opening up your way listed in *Adweek*: entry level, good illustration skills. What do you think?"

Irene was quiet a long moment, and when she spoke, it was in the language she assumed in her letters, clipped and cheerful, politely affectionate. So glad to know things are going well for him. How unfortunate that she could not be here to see him. But good luck! It was good of him to call, good of him to think of her, and he should really try to make himself at home. Merritt knows that was a sham. She is not so together as all that. Look at this place!

What he wants now is to root through her things in search of his own, the old irritation at her mess turned suddenly dear—to trail a lazy hand along the floor around the mattress, fishing for cigarettes, a pen, his socks. But his archaeology has long been unearthed. Brush away the layers, and he will find someone else's relics embedded in her new stratum. He shouldn't have come.

He doesn't have to look hard for evidence. A dry glaze of whiskers coats the bathroom sink, and when he opens the medicine cabinet, he sees that her tube of diaphragm jelly has been squeezed almost flat. There's just a pang at that, a small clench in his chest, which eases; he's figured on this, really. He just doesn't know how to respond, because in the way he played it out in his head, she is here to allude to it or confess it tearfully. He shakes her in anger or sits in mute, tight-lipped judgment. Either version ends with them making love in their fierce old way, all items swept aside to clear a surface. The den carpet, he thinks wistfully. It is plush and wouldn't burn his knees.

It occurs to Merritt that Irene has intended for him to see, that all of the mess was meant to seem like careless disclosure. He sifts though drawers. Somewhere she must keep her pictures of the two of them, at least one for nostalgia. That would somehow confirm her plotting, confirm that he is still important enough for Irene to want to hurt. There are bills, coupons, scissors and pens, greeting cards for all occasions, stray batteries and rubber bands, nothing telling. A cursory glance in her pantry reveals a backlog of shaped pastas and canned delicacies like artichoke hearts. The implication is clear to Merritt. Old Whiskers and Jelly is no mere one-night stand but in fact a well-fed lover! In revenge, Merritt could toss all these expensive tidbits into one big pot and boil them down to sticky hodgepodge. He instead pours himself a snifter of her good brandy, stored beneath the sink.

Irene is a generous hostess. In another time, in the kitchen not so unlike this one, she would be stocking-footed, stirring and simmering, offering Merritt spoonfuls of sauce and topping off his drink. Dinner would come late, and he would trace her collarbones with his brandied tongue, and she would open, open, open.

It is more than past his bedtime.

There is no one to set the unfamiliar alarm clock to go off at fifteen-minute intervals, but somehow Merritt wakes in plenty of time. Half dozing in bed at dawn, he thinks of dust, how he's read somewhere that over three-fourths of your common household variety is particles of human skin. Dust must coat every surface of Irene's apartment, and he has surely breathed it in all night from the curtains, from the pillow shams he neglected to change.

A dose of coffee and loud radio on the drive to the interview helps sponge his head clear of such thoughts, but once in the Formica-shiny checkerboard waiting area, Merritt detects the merest scent of Irene's pricey face cream, which he slathered on his beard before shaving.

He thumbs idly through his portfolio, second-guessing the choices he's made: copies of flyers and cassette covers designed for a friend's band, photos of a shop window he paints on Halloweens and Xmases, the best sketches from a medical-illustration class abandoned mid-semester. No rhyme or reason. But what else was there to show? Irene would call these "perfectly legitimate," "eclectic" even.

A man enters, obviously harried. He wears a rumpled blazer and jeans; they must be fairly casual here. That's a good thing; Merritt has only the one suit, and it feels forced, unnatural. The man thrusts his hand out to Merritt, who clutches it and quickly lets go. Too quickly? Well, if everything rests on a damn handshake, then who needs it anyway, right?

"Ron Claxton. And you must be my eight o'clock?"

"Merritt," says Merritt, in what he hopes is not too

corrective a tone. Still, he considers himself nobody's eight o'clock, and they may as well know it straightaway. He stands.

"Right this way, Merritt," says Ron, lightly palming the back of Merritt's shoulder to guide him along. Ron's office has the same slick tiling as the reception area, but on his chrome-looking desk are irreverent things like a Gumby with black voodoo pins stuck through its head and a gorilla face leering from a coffee mug. Merritt feels reassured by their presence and settles easily into the chair Ron gestures toward.

When Ron says, "So tell me about yourself," all the right deceptive words are waiting. Merritt's an earnest young man from a working-class family. He's got talent but had few good breaks. He's taking a brief hiatus from college; he hints that the reason is financial but is too proud to say so outright. This is the Merritt Irene used to present to her family and friends, and it does sound pretty good—Ron's face is rapt and softening. He flips through Merritt's portfolio with near tenderness, mur-muring appreciatively. Merritt knows his color wheel, knows his Gestalt—he's got the basics; he's raw talent brimming with potential. It amuses Merritt to appear finally to be embracing all this garbage when Irene will never know it.

"And what brings you so far from home?" Ron asks, affec-tion edging his voice. Merritt finds he has no ready answer to this, and the interview ends a little awkwardly. But promising, still very promising.

Isabelle and Violet Are Good Friends

Isabelle at fourteen has the habit of chewing at the hard corners of skin around her fingernails, though the nails themselves are intact and starting to grow long. She paints them red or black, then chips away at the polish to make it seem careless. It is the same with her jeans, chosen for their deliberate patterns of wear: they are stone, glacier, pepper, or acid washed; pebbled, used, or distressed; beaten or flogged. One brand of jeans, called Abused, boasts a technique called pummeling to distinctively mar the denim. Jagged fringe-edged tears run from hip to ankle, and it appears as though a sander has been taken to the knees and the seat. Isabelle would like a pair, but they cost fifty-eight dollars and your panties show if you wear them, which Isabelle does.

Violet does not, sometimes. Isabelle thinks this makes Violet decadent, and so they are good friends. At Isabelle's house after school, they sprawl out in beanbag chairs in front of the television and smoke. Isabelle's mom, Fran, doesn't care. Or she cares but has given up trying to make Isabelle do or not do anything. She does show a disproportionate amount of anger when they smoke her cigarettes, though, super-low-tar brands that they have to pinch the filter off to even taste. "Damn it, if you're going to smoke, you're going to buy your own!" she shrieks.

Isabelle has thirty shades of eye shadow, arranged in a black lacquer compact the shape of an artist's palette, a gift from her father's girlfriend. She daubs at the greens and golds with a sable brush, makes light sweeps across Violet's eyelids. Violet is an autumn, so earthier tones work best on her, but she insists on lining her eyes with thick navy pencil. She thinks it makes her eyes appear bluer, but Isabelle thinks it looks slutty, which she would never, ever say to Violet and hurt her feelings. Instead, she has asked to do Violet's makeup before they go out, confident that Violet will prefer the new, subtler look. She emphasizes the crease in Violet's eyelids with a smudgy line of forest green, highlights her brow bones with frosted bronze, then blends with the corner of a clean white sponge. She dusts Violet's face with translucent powder, then flicks her lashes lightly with mascara.

"Okay, open your eyes," she announces proudly. Violet blinks, preens before the compact mirror, then reaches as if instinctively for the navy pencil.

"I just need a little more definition," she explains.

Isabelle fumes but says nothing. She coats her own face with ivory matte primer, slicks on plum-red lipstick. Isabelle is a minimalist tonight. She wears black jeans, only mildly frayed, a black V-neck sweater, black boots. Her hair is crunchy blue-black from a cheap color rinse. She rakes her chipped red nails through her bangs, pulling them up and out, sprays them with Stiffy Hair Lacquer, which smells of apples.

Violet has run away, so she stays at Isabelle's house. This is allowed by Isabelle's mom, but for two weeks only. Violet's dad drinks. He turns on her suddenly and without remorse. Back talk gets stinging slaps, and once he prodded her in the ribs making some angry point, dotting her chest with small bruises. Mostly he just yells, but there is no telling how bad it will get; best to just get out of there. Last night Violet came home from the mall with a leather bustier and a hickey, and this did not set well with him. Her mother tried to stay out of it, but he eventually started in on her too, so Violet was able to slip away.

Isabelle's mom used to drink and so feels sorry for Violet, though uneasy about her bond with Isabelle. The girls seem sullen and capable of anything. They want nothing from her but shelter; no permission, no advice. Still, she can help them understand about the drinking, she thinks. She thinks she has that to offer. It is a disease, she tries to explain, but Isabelle is so sick of that refrain. She cuts her mother right off. Isabelle used to have to go to this support group for kids where they would say you can't hate them, it's a disease, you wouldn't hate somebody who had cancer, would you? Hate the disease, they said. It was all too abstract for Isabelle, hating the disease. Hate her mom, now that made perfect sense, but she doesn't anymore. She just does what she likes.

What Isabelle likes is to bring a boy right to his threshold, keep him pivoting there, her palm fastened to the lump in his jeans. This is power easily sustained, a little applied pressure, a sweep of the tongue behind the ear. She rotates the heel of her hand slowly, slowly, containing the wild swivel his hips attempt, letting his small spittly moans escape, his soft curses. The boy is young, and so desperate for impact he endures this. If he grows too insistent, she removes her palm altogether. She says she has to go home.

Violet will not touch boys there except lightly, as if by accident, but her boyfriend, Todd, has inserted his index finger in her up to the second knuckle. It felt like he could squish her insides, damage something, so she held very still and did not breathe until he withdrew it. She prefers to kiss, but Todd sucks on her tongue too hard sometimes, like he will pull it out at the root. She cannot tell him this, cannot imagine saying "suck" or "tongue" out loud to him, though she says far worse to Isabelle. She tells Todd, "Don't," but will not specify. She means all of it sometimes.

Todd meets them outside the movie theater, and Violet embraces him madly. Her father has told him not to show his butt around their house again, so their love has become suddenly, deliciously forbidden. Isabelle stands off to the side of the groping couple, smoking. She flicks her ashes toward them with quiet contempt.

She did not know Todd would be meeting them, though it is usually this way now. Violet will want Isabelle to go with her to a movie, a party, the mall, but their time together is only the time before, the getting-ready part, and after, when she spends the night. All the in-between time is with Todd, who meets them places and makes out with Violet as if Isabelle is not even there. There used to be a sort of agreement between the girls that they would never do this to each other. But that was months ago, when their friendship was something different. Back then they decided it was tacky and disloyal to leave your friend while you make out with some boy. At the time, though, it had been Isabelle meeting all the boys.

Todd and Violet retract their tongues and separate. Todd stares blankly at Isabelle, who meets his eyes for a brief angry flash before shifting her gaze to just over his shoulder.

"What's up," he says to her, not a question. Isabelle gives a single nod in response. He is ugly! she thinks, with his blotchy red face and his knobby Adam's apple. Violet says he breaks out because he has to shave, as if that makes bad skin a more admirable trait. And he is far too skinny, the way his Levi's sag. Isabelle has been with far better than this. Violet could be too, but Violet settles.

Todd and Violet want to go into the theater, so Isabelle waves them on, wanting to finish her cigarette. She shivers in her thin sweater, feeling suddenly very foolish for refusing the jacket her mom suggested. But she cannot afford to indulge the woman, cannot give on anything. It feels like any adult could confront her now—*What do you think you are doing?* meaning her hair, her smoking, her clothes—and she would be defenseless, ducking her head in shame, murmuring excuses.

Violet meets her in the dark aisle of the theater. "Come with me to the bathroom," she urges Isabelle, who shakes her head no: "I want to see the previews."

Violet squeezes her hand. "I am the happiest," she whispers. "Tell you later." She sprints away to touch up her eyeliner.

Isabelle sits next to Todd and watches light flicker greenly across his expressionless face, watches him feed popcorn into his mouth piece by piece. He has asked Violet to *go with him*, no doubt, an expression Isabelle despises. What does it mean? More access, probably. She eases her hand up his leg and nudges his crotch. He jerks in slight surprise at her touch, then moves the greasy popcorn bucket over his lap, presses it down on her hand. Cartoon cups of soda, Hershey bars, and Jujy fruits line dance Rockette-style across the screen. *Visit the concession stand!* they urge. When Violet returns, Isabelle is licking butter from her knuckles. Todd shifts uneasily in his seat. *Shh! Keep it quiet!* caution the dancing snacks.

Isabelle turns fifteen and starts waiting tables evenings after school and weekends at Marlo's, a family-style restaurant with all-booth seating. She has to wear a hair net, clunky nurse shoes, and a crisp red multipocketed apron for keeping her tips and tickets straight. If the dishwashers didn't share their pot, the job would be unbearable. She smokes a little with them out back by the dumpsters before her shift, then drizzles her eyes with Visine, chews cinnamon gum, and slips on the ridiculous hair net. Stoned, it's not as difficult to be in strangers' faces, smiling while they order her around and complain about the food she brings them, or how slow she is to refill their drinks and clear the table. She pokes along dreamily, feeling outside all the suppertime clamor and haste. The night manager, a plump, jittery college student, grows suspicious and nagging, but

Isabelle doubts he will do anything. He is rendered helpless, outnumbered by young waitresses in clingy knit skirts.

Violet's parents will not allow her to work until she turns sixteen, which is fine with her. She is also not allowed to date until then, but she comes home early enough on school nights now, books under her arm, to avoid confrontation. Her mother has negotiated a shaky peace between Violet and her father, one built on mutual fear. Violet tries not to provoke him so he will keep his violence in check, and he tries not to provoke her for fear she will get pregnant or a venereal disease out of spite. The calm in their household is tenuous at best. Drinking, her father maintains a membrane-thin semblance of control. And Violet remains a virgin, though also membrane-thin.

But she is *going with* Todd now, and she feels this lends her some of the same mature, distancing qualities she would have if she were having actual sex. She feels vibrantly grown and credible bringing him to Marlo's to eat fudge cake and order Isabelle around. "Oh, miss!" she mocks her friend. "Service, please!" In this small way, Violet exacts revenge. For what, she isn't quite sure, but it is highly satisfying.

Isabelle smiles at her indulgently, while a fist pulses in her stomach. *Just keep on*, she thinks. Every little injustice becomes a favor she will lavish on Todd when he meets her in the restaurant parking lot at closing time, past Violet's curfew. In his father's old Thunderbird, so wide she can lie down flat in the seat, she will kiss him with such ferocity that their tongues will ache.

Todd is good practice for Isabelle. He assumes an air of shy, amused embarrassment at the restaurant, but nothing more.

Around Violet, Isabelle is just the friend of his girlfriend. Isabelle mirrors his feigned indifference. She has tapped into some secret code of behavior that makes her capable of intrigues and treachery. She wants to try this with other boys, with men, but something still nags at her. She is afraid the indifference is real, afraid of just barely seeming to exist to someone who has touched her. When this no longer matters, Isabelle feels she can go on to someone else. Todd is good practice.

Stoned, sleepy, Isabelle navigates the dining room with a coffeepot in each hand, one regular, one decaf. She is supposed to make a round with the water pitcher as well, but it seems that nobody drinks from the tiny glasses she has to bring them. They want soda or iced tea, then coffee afterward. It is just an empty gesture of hospitality, bringing the water. Marlo's server-training filmstrip admitted as much, but it is policy nonetheless.

There are certain steps she must follow here. She must greet her customers with hearty earnestness, presenting them with water glasses and cutlery within minutes of their arrival. She must have a working knowledge of the menu and be able to recite the evening's specials on command. She must shamelessly hawk the desserts. Employees from the Marlo's chain corporate office are purported to disguise themselves as regular customers and eat there, then fill out a form describing all the server's shortcomings. Isabelle is not too worried about this happening. She omits none of the prescribed steps, though she has a bit of difficulty with the hearty earnestness part. This is why her manager is uneasy. It will not do to have distracted or irreverent servers. It is certain to reflect on him.

When Isabelle's assigned section finally clears some, he summons her to his "office," a small square of space in the kitchen, set off by metal shelves of huge canned vegetables, condiment refills, and soup base. The dishwashers snicker as she walks past. "*Busted*," one calls to her softly, an oily boy in a Metallica T-shirt. Isabelle used to think he was scummy cute, but he acts too disgusting. She sticks her tongue out and he goes wild, whooping, making jack-off gestures with his fist.

"Give it a rest, Marty," calls the manager from behind the shelves. He sits on an overturned mop bucket, pretending to take silent inventory of the shelves' contents. When Isabelle appears, he gestures at a step stool. "Have a seat." She does, adjusting her skirt primly.

"I was just wondering, um, if there was, you know, a problem or something," he says, his gaze shifting from the shelves to Isabelle's smooth rounded knees encased in tan nylon, then quickly back to the shelves.

"No," she says in mock wonder. "Why? Am I doing something wrong?" She purses her lips in pretty, petulant concern, leans forward intently.

He blurts, "No, no! I mean, well, there's just something . . ." He grapples, then finds the words. "You just seem distracted." He sighs. That is more like what he wants to say. "Distracted," he repeats with emphasis, hoping to infuse the word with deeper meaning.

"Oh," she replies, then leans back. "Is that it?" The thick rubber sole of her shoe makes impatient smacking sounds.

"Well, yes. I mean, is there anything wrong?"

"Are people complaining about me?" she demands.

"No!" he exclaims, louder than he means to, suddenly agonizingly aware of his erection pressing against the zippered fly of his khaki chinos, there partly from nervousness, partly from his close proximity to Isabelle. She sees it too.

"I've got to clean up," she tells it, barely suppressing her smirk, then leaves. For the remainder of the evening, she does not serve water unless it is specifically requested. If customers ask about the specials, she directs their attention to the blackboard. She confesses that the crumb cake is dry and mealy, the cheesecake an insubstantial sliver for $2.95. Isabelle has achieved job security.

Isabelle finishes a big cup of grape Kool-Aid and clear liquor she can barely taste, and Violet dips her another one out of a red plastic cooler. They don't know whose house this is, loud and jammed with people, coiled radiators spewing heat. Todd has a sixth sense about parties, finds one nearly every weekend. He drove both Violet and Isabelle to this one in the Thunderbird, an awkward arrangement. Violet rode shotgun, official under the crook of his arm, while Isabelle glowered in the back seat, letting cigarette ash drip all over, remembering how the hot vinyl had sucked at her skin.

It's easy to gulp down the Kool-Aid, sweet and cold. Isabelle dips herself another cupful. She dances on the cracked kitchen linoleum, mostly small rhythmic pulses of her shoulders and hips, and she knows the neck of her tunic is drifting over to one side, showing the satiny black strap of her bra. A boy in a college sweatshirt, blond-haired, cute, tries to dance with her, but he can only ape her mincing steps. After a few minutes, he gives up, shouts, "You are *so* pretty!" over the music, and they kiss. It is no good; his tongue lolls thick and foreign in her mouth, which is coated with the sticky-sweet punch. It is so hot in the kitchen, and where is Violet? Isabelle pulls away to get a refill and light a cigarette. When she turns back, the boy is gone. She resumes her small dance alone, careful not to spill her drink.

It creeps up on her, pulling her head down heavy and dull, a squirmy unfolding feeling in her stomach. She nudges her way through the tight press of bodies, angry because it is too hot and loud here and she knows no one but Violet and Todd, who are sharing a joint in the corner, their backs to her. She tugs the single beaded braid in Violet's long hair, hating it and her.

"I'm ready to go," Isabelle demands, but her voice is small and wan, not what she intends. She can't wait for an answer. She careens back to the kitchen and finds the phone, fumbles with the rotary dial. She cannot tell her mother to come quickly enough—the urgent lurch in her belly, mouth filling with wet. She retches vibrant purple in the sink, and people back off, clearing the kitchen. When the wave passes, some-one—not Violet—helps her to the cold front steps. Her eyes moisten and burn.

Sick, waiting, she decides she will let Todd have sex with her the next time they are alone together. She'd like to see the look on his face then! Try being aloof—try not noticing, Violet. See if you can pretend then. If she bleeds, it will sponge off the vinyl car seat easily, leaving no trace, but they all will know that something irrevocable has happened. Isabelle will not be ignored. She wonders if her mother will be able to find her.

Isabelle's mother sits in the dank cellar of a church, wincing at the clang of metal folding chairs being arranged in a circle. She tamps her cigarette into the coffee-dampened Styrofoam cup squeezed between her knees, waits for the settling in. When her turn comes, she exclaims, "I'm Fran and I'm an alcoholic!" and everyone responds, "Hey, Fran!" with genuine warmth. They swap stories and stirring mottos. *Easy does it. Just for today.* They're simple, effective, and meaningful, as few things are.

Fran's stories are embarrassing and funny, a great hit. She put the station wagon in a half-dozen soft ditches, got fired from one job for mouthing off at the boss, another for coming in hungover and puking in a potted plant. She'd been somewhat of a gymnast in college, but no more. Bearing down on forty, drinking, drunk, she felt a false suppleness in her joints one night and tried to rise from the floor in a backbend. A segment in her spine dislodged, and she spent the next three months in a torso cast. Her husband, Isabelle's father, kept her prescriptions filled and the bar well stocked. He was her Enabler, she has told the group, the one who dulled her pain so he could keep inflicting it.

That's not entirely fair. There were some shoves and a slap, which she suspects she coaxed out of him, one brief remorse-filled affair, and she had held him to those things for four impossible years. The words that sprang from her mouth then!

Misery made her sharp and clever in a way she still sometimes craves, like the tang on her palate from cheap white wine, from gin. On Saturday nights, for forever it seemed, her husband had grilled thick red steaks and pawed at her in front of Isabelle.

"Your mama's gonna be sorry she ever met me tonight," he drawled to their daughter in a too-sexy voice one steak night; Isabelle was around nine. He swatted Fran's rear with a dish towel, waggled a two-pronged meat fork with friendly menace.

"I already *am* sorry I ever met you," was her reply, and it was funny; even Isabelle laughed. Her husband did not laugh; he no longer found Fran amusing. He squeezed Fran's wrist too hard, jerking her toward him. "You think you can just trash me in front of her?" he demanded, and Isabelle was of course right there watching even then; it was very near the end.

Fran never hit Isabelle, nor did she allow her husband to; she cannot emphasize this enough.

Earl M., a carpenter who has fifteen years of sobriety, gives Fran a slow wink and a smile. She cried in his arms once after a meeting and still bristles from the feel of another man's body. He had less bulk to him than Isabelle's father, and the intimate press of their bones stays with her. They will only have coffee together, though, and she will speak to him in quiet, wondrous tones of her daughter, who has sprung away from her with such force that she can only watch her go. There's something about that in the Serenity Prayer, accepting things you can't change.

Fran's ex-husband, Leonard, has a girlfriend, Elizabeth, pretty and wan and so young it still smarts for Fran to look at her. Elizabeth comes with Leonard to take Isabelle out to dinner, to the movies, or away for the weekend, and it is relief mixed with pain for Fran to see the three together, a tidy little family unit, all smiles for one another. As the part-time parent, Leonard gets to be the good guy now: no hassles, all pleasant outings and special meals. Elizabeth gets to be Isabelle's confidante, an older-sister type who is eager to be liked. She teaches Isabelle to drive and lends her clothes; Isabelle has her pager number. Fran knows she should be glad, but isn't. She thinks of all she doesn't know about her own daughter and resents what might be shared with Leonard's girlfriend.

Probably, though, Isabelle confides in no one except Violet, a girl Fran alternately likes and pities; she is troubled and sneaky and barely to be trusted. Her heavy makeup and sexy clothes suggest a disturbing, precocious knowledge, but she cries easily and often turns to Fran for comfort. The thought of trying to separate the two friends, even to protect Isabelle, cuts at Fran, makes her relent, forgive, even trust a little in what the girls have together.

Many from the group are gathering at a waffle shop, which they often do after weekend meetings. Earl M. asks Fran if she's going, and she hesitates, wanting his company. But she wants to be home more; it's Saturday night, and she's thinking of her daughter, a guilty twinge, though she feels sure Isabelle isn't thinking of her. Something nags, though; she should be home in case. Always in case. There could be a needful call, or Isabelle might come home heartbroken, and Fran might soothe her, filling the doorway of her daughter's bedroom with attentiveness and care, not daring to go in. It's the least, the very least, she might offer.

If nothing else, that would lend some interest to another weekend spent sober. Fran is becoming accustomed to a dull, undefined worry about what Isabelle might be doing, since it is rarely revealed. Otherwise, there are only the meetings, rented movies, and tea or coffee with the other divorced ex-drinkers. None of the wildness of the old days. Fran remembers digging out an old girdle to help squeeze her leftover pregnant paunch into a slinky strapless dress when Isabelle was two months old, working a party with the baby on her hip, her free hand cradling a wineglass.

Fran and her husband had been attractive and popular, and she hadn't been about to change that much over a baby. Fran had loved to the brink of desperation Isabelle's tiny little face, her soft baby chub, but had not been prepared for the neediness. It was drink that made her lazy and selfish—Fran knew it even then—but a child was exhausting no matter what you did. She'd gotten so impatient for Isabelle to learn to talk, to walk, to feed and dress herself, she'd pushed her toward moments where Fran's every fiber didn't have to focus on her. If Fran's attention strayed too much, Isabelle could choke or wham her soft head on the fireplace. She could get lost, hungry, wet, her shoelaces dangling helplessly, hurtling her down dark stairwells into the arms of strangers. But such things seem small now to Fran, utterly preventable. Her daughter has entered new realms of danger. Fran is seized by new currents of dread, and these are what carry her home early, quickly, ready.

Of course, she is right; she is just in time for the call. A Mother's Intuition, is what she will tell her AA friends. Isabelle stranded and God knows what all else at a party: Fran fears only the worst would compel her daughter to call her for help. Soon Fran is driving downtown in search of the vague address given her. The bars near the university are filled to bursting, people are spilling out onto the sidewalks in drunken waves. The names of the bars have changed, but Fran remembers these places all too well, filled with dank warmth and throbby music and dark possibilities. Isabelle is mature-looking for her age. Enough makeup and cleavage would likely get her into any of them, no questions asked.

Fran finds the low-numbered north end of the street she is looking for and turns into a residential area. The farther south she drives, the wider the gaps between streetlights, the murkier and more crumbling the houses. Her daughter crying out to her from one of them—it makes Fran's pulse leap, her hands tremble on the wheel, foot twitching from gas to brake to gas, making the car lurch uncertainly forward. Isabelle could barely have avoided the weakness, Fran thinks. It is too much for her to be fifteen, alcohol and drugs everywhere she turns. Two drunks for parents and Isabelle not touched by it? Impossible. It is the same pull, the same sway and bliss Fran knew, but Isabelle will not hear it from Fran. She has her heart shut tight against this knowledge. Still, it is Fran that she called, not her father or Elizabeth.

Fran detects the muffled throb of music and knows she is near. The house is easy enough to spot: porch lights on, cars all over the lawn and along the curb. A girl sits on the sagging front steps, head down between her knees, hands clasped around the nape of her neck. Fran recognizes the tufted hair, the familiar black boots, as belonging to Isabelle. She brakes, puts the car in park, and idles there, not wanting to approach the house. She taps the horn tentatively, then longer. Isabelle lifts her head, drops it down again.

The front door opens and Violet emerges, cup in hand, from the crushed blur of bodies within the house. She sits beside Isabelle, slides an arm along her shoulders, and leans in to offer her a drink of water. Isabelle shakes her head, keeping it down. Fran taps the horn again.

Violet looks up and waves. She coaxes Isabelle to her feet, and Isabelle lurches down the steps. Fran unlocks the passenger door as Violet propels Isabelle toward the car.

"She's really messed up," Violet tells Fran apologetically, easing Isabelle into the seat. "I offered to get Todd to drive her home, but she said no way. I guess she called you, huh?"

"She been drinking?" Fran asks, unnecessarily. The acrid smell steams off Isabelle, who drops her head back down between her knees.

"Yeah," Violet says, her face blank innocence.

"Have you?" Fran asks. "You need a ride?"

"No; no, thanks. I can be out till one tonight."

Fran watches Violet's red, red mouth and marvels at how easily these girls look her in the face and lie. "You did this," she tells her coldly, knowing it isn't true; Isabelle does what she likes. Violet shrugs. She's where she doesn't give a damn, soft and floaty. Fran recognizes the look, feels a small tug of worry, but decides to let Violet be somebody else's problem tonight. "Be careful," she admonishes her, and leaves it at that.

"I want you to sit up and put your seat belt on," Fran informs Isabelle, all business, when they are back on the main road heading home. No response from Isabelle, but she can hear her full heavy breaths.

"Isabelle, sit up!" Now that she knows her daughter is relatively unharmed, Fran can start to get angry. Grabbing the back of her shirt, she jerks her upright. Isabelle flails back like a rag doll, moaning.

"I don't understand you." Fran sighs. "Is this what you want to be? You can't do this and go on living with me." Time for sternness. Tough love. House rules.

Isabelle can't answer; she is struggling to keep the bile beneath her throat. Her pores exude poison.

"I mean it, Isabelle! I'll pack your shit tonight!"

"Gonna be sick," Isabelle warns, head lolling forward.

"Damn it! Hold on!" shouts Fran, swerving over to the side of the road. Vomit spatters Isabelle's boots, the floor, before Fran can lunge across, open the door, and shove her in the direction of the grass. Isabelle kneels, still heaving, feeling the foulness surging out. When it ebbs, her lips puff "Mom," so softly she doesn't think Fran can hear.

"Let your father deal with this," Fran tells Isabelle's shuddering back. "I can't take this." But her voice turns crooning, and she strokes her daughter's neck and shoulders. "I can't take this, baby."

PRODIGY

What Jasper can't get over are her miniature hands: blue-veined and corded as an old woman's; the expert positioning of the fingers, now nimbly dancing, now muscled blunt against the strings. Her delicate grip on the bow, carving sound, invokes a stiff rhythmic sway in her body, precise as a metronome. Those hands, and yet her face is baby sleek and rounded, two spots of color dabbed high on the plump cheeks. Her tiny pursed mouth is rouged blood red. They paint her face but dress her as a child. The high-waisted yellow dress lies smooth and flat across her chest, crinoline peeps from her fanned skirt; her colt-legged spindly stance is anchored in black buckled shoes.

Gwendolyn Kim is a child, ten years old, but small even for ten, barely four feet tall. Exquisitely tiny! Her violin is toy-sized. She has been playing since she was four, touring since age seven. She is the child of Korean refugees, their miracle in

America. It is a miracle, too, that Jasper has found her, that random channel flipping landed him this. God bless public TV's middle-of-the-night eclecticism. Mild interest held him through the six-year-old math whiz and the eleven-year-old medical student—until Gwendolyn Kim. Her ancient hands and soft baby body, her painted face and little-girl dress, thrill and confuse him. He feels her aura penetrate the sickly green rays of the television and infuse him with a pure light. What he feels he can only call rapture.

Nothing enraptures Jasper in this town. He saves money for the Big Move but suspects it will never happen. His plans are too ill-conceived, too vague. He knows only that he wants to go away—to a city, perhaps—but he hates traffic and noise. He hates not knowing his way around. The rent on his claustrophobic studio apartment is an unsurpassed bargain. The thrift in him cannot bear to pay more.

Gwendolyn Kim flies to Chicago, New York, Minneapolis, Topeka. Her tours are interior. She is whisked from plane to car to hotel, where she pockets the small tablets of soap. She is combed, fitted and painted, then jettisoned to the dark caverns of music halls.

Jasper spends the money he's saved on MUS 110—Music Appreciation—at the university. He learns Baroque from Classical. He buys a candle in the shape of a treble clef. He buys a poster that he lacks the courage to hang. It is of a pointed ballet shoe balancing on a bow, stark against the curved silhouette of a violin. *Adagio*, it says in gold across the bottom. *Slow in tempo.*

It is the way things move in this town, slow in tempo. One season drags reluctantly into the next. The shopping mall forms one brick at a time amid ownership disputes. It remains an unfulfilled promise of a food patio raucous with teenagers and shops that sell funky ethnic bracelets. The students don't believe. They desert the town every weekend and all summer long, and they never look back. The university is rigid ancient limestone, grounded in its own perpetuity. Plaques on fountains speak of a grim century, a modest birth as a teachers college and growth into a "humanities stronghold." Jasper feels he conceded to something when he paid for his three credit hours. Perhaps it is just the new vocabulary: *tuition, elective, bursar, syllabus, transcript.*

Jasper rides his bike to the columned auditorium two mornings a week for his music lecture, then to Rollo's, where he replenishes the salad bar (*Smorgas!* in shiny brass letters overhead) and wipes down tables. Rollo's every day. From midafternoon on, people collect around the bar, noisy, rude, furiously drinking. They spill more liquor than they drink, and they polish off heaping platters of chicken wings and nachos. By two-thirty or three A.M., they ebb, leaving the surfaces gluey as flypaper.

Gwendolyn Kim's days are rigid with discipline, allowing only for excellence, nothing clumsy or superfluous. She is fed on gruel, nutritious but bland. Flavors could distract. No television; a private tutor who speaks in monotone. She sleeps in her velvet-lined violin case, a brick of rosin closed in each tiny fist. Her head must be a resonant chamber, a conduit for music.

A couple or five beers, and Jasper heads home. He tries to listen to the tapes from class, but the sounds elude him dreamily, sifting through his head and gone. He turns on Hank Williams or the baseball game. It is only Gwendolyn Kim's playing that captivates him. He eats a soggy melted ham and cheese sandwich out of its Styrofoam box. He rakes the bottom of a potato chip bag for salty crumbs. He tips back a waxy cup of soda, feels it coat his teeth with stickiness.

What is talent? Jasper's mother keeps his rude crayon drawings and a plaster cast of his small hands to commemorate an average childhood. Jasper Leonard Shoemacher. Ten fingers and ten toes. His halting recitation of the ABCs. The tying of the shoelaces. Big hand on the twelve, little hand on the six; six o'clock is suppertime. Ate all his broccoli, didn't like tuna fish. Loved canned pears and beef jerky. Fingerprints in the margarine, greasy mouth proclaiming innocence. Plucked at his genitals, but the doctor said fine, fine. The cowlick splayed at a defiant angle, resisting wet combs and hair spray. Cursive and times tables on the dry brown paper. Strep throat and chicken pox. A broken wrist. Going with a girl, freckles and gray eyes, who plunged her tongue into his mouth, sixth grade. His fingers traced the elastic of her bra, but the teacher found them in the spring-damp woods beyond the soccer fields. Drafting class, English lit, track team that ended with the cigarettes. Growth, urging and insistent, aching in his thighbones. Bumps red and painful, Adam's apple jutting like a beak. Best friend Phil, who lit his own farts to make a blue flame and got them sweet red wine to drink. No girls since that first one; eighteen and still no girls! His head brimmed with heat and longing. The whore, his age or younger, eyes crusty with mascara, opened beneath him, and he shriveled inside her. Saw her emptying the trash when he left. The Tokyo Sauna, open twenty-four hours, still red, winking neon beyond town, an embarrassment still. For eight years he guns the motor past.

Gwendolyn Kim coats her tongue with the soap, waggles it at her tutor. See? Too sick to play tonight. When she is sick, she gets to wear her flannel pajamas and drink hot chicken broth. She is given two vitamin C pills and holds them sour in her mouth until they burn. The draperies are closed and the tapes are shut off, so it is blissfully quiet and she can rest. But today the tutor shakes her head ruefully. The jig is up: she sees the foam edging Gwendolyn Kim's lips. "Shame! Everyone is expecting you."

Is lighting your own farts a talent? Is whoring? Jasper can slice a radish paper thin; he can maneuver his bike between snugly parked cars. The music class, he learns, is considered a "blow-off." Nobody goes to the listening lab. The tests are true-false and multiple choice. They are required to attend three musical performances, but people nab the programs for evidence and leave at intermission. The professor is hapless and kind. He ignores the frank snores and plays an assortment of instruments—so far the oboe, the accordion, and the bagpipes. No strings, though, no violin. Jasper doggedly attends each lecture, even after the caterwauling bagpipes caused him to clasp the sides of his head. Is doggedness a talent?

In the murmuring dark, in the amniotic wings, Gwendolyn Kim waits. Her accompanist, another of the great gray pianists who change from city to city, fumbles with the buttons on his vest, claps his big meaty hand down on her shoulder before shuffling out onto the stage, only the tiny glow of the lamp over his sheet music to guide him. But Gwendolyn Kim steps out into a circle of light, violin nestled in the crook of her arm. There are restrained smatterings of applause; they are wary of her size and so reserve their enthusiasm. They are curious, they are doubting; she is too wee and adorable. They expect only to be charmed.

At the lip of the stage, she peers down at the shadowy audience, imagining their expectant maws. Mess up, and in you go, she tells herself. They will devour you with pity. She slides a foot sideways, then forward slightly, inching her toes ahead to test the edge. She swings her violin up and fits her chin into the rest, clears her throat expectantly, the bow poised. The piano tinkles feebly behind, and she razors, wings beating furiously, the bow a zigzag, a stabbing. Her forearms thrum, protract. Her wrist palpitates blood to the fingers, the fingers leap and press with programmed certainty. Then slowly she sears the strings, a distended moan.

Jasper skips out on the jazz ensemble (number two of the three) at intermission. At the entrance, his professor leans against a pillar, smoking.

"Did you remember your program?" he quips to Jasper, who unclasps and scrambles onto his bike. No time for irony. Rollo's, then home.

Once
Removed

⁓⁓⁓

When Marta falls asleep, sometimes she is engulfed by sound. It begins as a soft, curious whirring and buzzing on the blurred edge of a dream, swells into a great roaring din that fills her head. It has some of the rough-hewn texture of a voice but is below the surface of a scream. It has the elusive quality of a glimpse; she is certain that if she can wrench herself awake, it will be gone. The surface of the bed tilts and pivots. She tries to force her eyelids open, but they balk at the effort, giving a bit, then snapping back tautly. The exertion further traps her, and she lies helpless beneath layers of sleep, immobile, clenched.

In the daytime, there is work to go to. There Marta gazes endlessly into a black screen, typing in various sets of numbers, the names of certain people, other facts with no meaning. There is a girl who sometimes sits on the same row, humming quietly to music on her headphones. Often she will join Marta in the break room. Although Marta prefers to brood quietly over her coffee, she says nothing to discourage her. She fears the look of puzzled hurt the girl would give her, then the hardening of her face as she gathers her knitting and moves to another table. Marta might then find she no longer likes the solitude that normally surrounds her. She feels this change already. When she comes to work, her ears prickle with anticipation of the girl's greeting. "Morning!" the girl shouts over her music. Sometimes Marta manages to say it back. When her throat goes dry, she just smiles.

The cat cringes from Marta lately. He presses himself against the wall, eyeing her warily as she pours the dry brown pellets into his bowl. He hesitates until she leaves the kitchen, darting across the floor only when she is safely out of view. Yesterday Marta found the remains of a crocheted doily he'd chewed and clawed to tatters. She wrapped it carefully in tissue and slid it into a drawer. The little yarn mouse she had brought him lay untouched, nestling safely by her slippers. She vaguely misses the sleekness and warmth of her cat. The apartment is cold nights, and she senses the absence of him curled against her belly. She must have slighted him in some way, she has been so distracted lately. She regrets this, as he does not forgive easily. She leaves him tiny saucers of milk as peace offerings, enticements. What she will do if he returns to her, she

does not know. She seems to lack the energy to keep from of-
fending him.

It is getting more difficult to look at the girl from work.
She tries to get acquainted with Marta. She asks pointed questions: "Where did you get your blouse?" "Isn't work a pain?"
"Do you like the city?" Today it was: "What do you do for fun?"
Marta froze. Any response seemed dangerous. To reply "Nothing" seemed most honest, but she feared the girl's pity. To
pretend a hobby seemed treacherous, and Marta never felt
competent enough for lies. In her panic, she murmured, "I have
a cat," though even that hardly seemed true anymore.

The girl seemed to believe it. "Really?" she said sweetly. "I
love cats. But my landlady won't let me keep one."

"Mine won't either," Marta half whispered, and they
grinned at each other conspiratorially. It felt wonderful, but
Marta feared the girl might somehow sense that thing in her
that the cat did and shrink from her also. Her smile faded, and
she looked down into her coffee, hardly daring to listen to the
girl as she relentlessly chatted on, something about dancing and
a small club, never having anyone to go with, tea and egg rolls,
peppermint schnapps.

The bell signaling the end of break clanged, jolting Marta
out of her malaise. The girl was folding a square of paper. She
tucked it into Marta's hand and left.

Trembling, Marta unfolded the paper. Written there in a
small, delicate hand was the girl's name and phone number. She
mouthed the name silently: *Alice*.

. . .

At home, Marta finds herself appalled by her careless assortment of furniture: a fat green couch with most of its stuffing poking out, a crooked red armchair that will not tilt back (the *decliner*, she called it), a coffee table of steel bars and cracked glass top, an unwieldy floor lamp looming dangerously over it all. A shelf in the corner holds bright enameled things: piggy banks, coffee mugs, ashtrays; relics of garage sales and dead relatives. *Alice* could never come here, see this. *Alice* probably had roomfuls of brass and wicker, dark polished woods, and colorful blankets she'd knitted over a thousand break times folded neatly over her couch, hanging on her walls, spread across her bed. *Alice*. It is strange to attach a name to her.

The naked bulb in Marta's bathroom gives off a harsh light, and she squints, trying to discern her face in the mirror. Its ruddiness is exaggerated in the cruel light, and her gray eyes and thin lips are lost in the mottled landscape. Her thick pale hair is uncontrollable. She tries to trap it in a bun for work, but by the end of the day it escapes from the clip and pokes out of her scalp in varied frizzy lengths. Alice has hair that is soft and brown and hangs to her shoulders in neat straight lines. Her face is smooth and tanned from careful makeup. Mascara shapes her long eyelashes into delicate points.

Marta could call; the phone number is safe in the pocket of her skirt. It is easier, though, to make toast and spread it with a thin layer of strawberry jam, take small, furtive bites. She leaves it, half eaten, on the nightstand and switches off the lamp. She waits for sleep. The cat lurks elsewhere in the apartment. She has left her bedroom door open; maybe he will decide to join her.

With sleep comes the chaos of sound and motion. She welcomes it at first; it will keep her from dreaming. But her last full thought is of drowning as she goes under.

Morning comes only by the sheer force of will, Marta thinks. She senses the new light in the room and struggles to get out to it. She jolts herself awake, sits straight up, tossing the bedclothes aside.

She is hurried and clumsy getting ready for work. Bits of tissue cling to her legs where she has nicked them shaving. Her hair is still slick with shampoo after the brisk rinsing, but that will help keep it in place, she rationalizes, jerking the wet mass into a clip. She devours a cold, crumbly biscuit, gulps her juice, and flings the glass into the sink. It shatters on impact, further alienating the cat, who flees the kitchen without breakfast.

Marta is sprinting to the bus stop, when she realizes she is not late. It is anticipation that makes her rush. She is anxious to speak with this new friend, share smiles with her.

Marta must calm down as she enters the building. She has become wary of her enthusiasm and doesn't want to worry Alice with it. She must slow down, gather her senses as she steps into the elevator, presses the button for the fifth floor. She must relax. She feels her stomach lurch and drop as the elevator ascends. She mustn't let her hands shake, or people will stare. She grips her purse tightly to steady them.

Alice isn't there yet, though she is usually early. It is five minutes to eight, so Marta slips silently down the second row to her desk and logs on to the computer. The new supervisor, a dour woman who wears drab, loose-fitting smocks, approaches her wordlessly, deposits a stack of papers on her desk. Today the smock is olive and made of a thick, woolly knit. *Gabardine*, Marta guesses, thumbing through the stack.

They must be updating the mailing list today. The papers are a mix of torn envelopes, invoices, and printouts from other companies. Marta sorts them accordingly and begins to alphabetize the names on the envelopes. She is wasting time, she realizes, but isn't ready to begin yet. She knows she will become transfixed, staring into the void of the computer screen, and might miss Alice's arrival.

At 8:25, Marta starts entering the names and addresses. She can't wait any longer; the supervisor keeps constant vigil and is starting to look suspicious. Marta must focus her attention on the data to avoid error. Other thoughts become peripheral as she types. She chants the words silently to herself as she enters them. Marta is an excellent typist. The pads of her fingers move swiftly across the keyboard, touching keys with lightness and accuracy. It is a skill she has performed for so long that it does not occur to her to be proud of it. Still, she wishes she could do everything with that same easy grace.

Eons later, a bell signals lunch. Alice's cubicle is still empty. Marta proceeds to the break room. She fills a Styrofoam cup with coffee and decides to take it outside to the courtyard, where there are benches and a goldfish pond. It is still cold, so perhaps no one else will be out there. The supervisor gestures at her vaguely with a cigarette as Marta leaves.

Outside, the sun is shining, but the wind is fierce, biting. Marta rebuttons her thin cardigan and shivers. The pond has been drained and is shallower than she'd thought; no more than a foot or two deep. The rocks that line the sides and the bottom are jagged and blackened by algae. She extends a cautious foot and dislodges a rock from the side, leaving a pocket in the soil where it was embedded. She wonders what they do with the fish all winter, imagines them stored in a freezer, waiting for spring to come. Would they be asleep, she wonders, aware of being trapped motionless?

Maybe Alice quit, she thinks. Maybe *she'll* quit. The thought of having to go back up there makes her feel suddenly angry. She could just leave now, go home, not even face that glowering old smock again. Go home, get reconciled with the cat, call Alice. Perhaps the cat would like it if she invited Alice over; then there would be two of them to play with him. He would likely prefer Alice to gloomy old Marta. If so, she'd give him to Alice. The very thought of this selfless act makes her wince with pleasure. That was the very sort of thing a true friend would do. She would try not to make a big deal out of it.

The planning has gone too far, Marta realizes. She has just seriously considered quitting her job and giving her cat to a near stranger, who would only laugh at the gesture. "Jeez, I was just trying to be friendly." She imagines Alice snickering. "I didn't mean for you to do *this*."

Marta begins to feel self-conscious sitting in the cold, empty courtyard, gazing dumbly at a barren fish pond. She wonders if anyone has seen her kick the rock loose. She goes back inside, climbs the stairs slowly, pausing at each landing for a ten count to use up the rest of her lunchtime.

Once, when she was too young, Marta's mother gave her a very expensive bracelet. It was made of silver and bits of an iridescent blue shell—called *paua*, she remembered. She spent much time admiring the colorful swirly patterns of the shell, hardly believing she possessed such a thing. The clasp made a marvelous clicking sound, and she fastened and unfastened it over and over again, until it finally broke. Her mother put it away until Marta was old enough to take care of her things properly. She never got it back. She figures this is fair.

At home, the cat is yowling pitifully. He has been batting at the broken glass fragments in the sink until one finally sliced his paw. Marta coos sympathetically and leans in to inspect the wound, but he hisses and spits at her. She backs away, palms out in supplication, murmuring apologies. A last resentful mew escapes as he runs from the room. Tiny spots of blood mark his trail. A shame about the glass, Marta thinks as she sponges up the mess. It was the last of a set belonging to an aunt who kept only beautiful things. It was tall and slim, delicately etched with flowers. She is so careless. Something in her, once deliberately caring, has died. She continues to clean the house, court the cat, only out of habit. He must be able to smell this.

The phone rings shrilly, unbelievably. Marta freezes a moment, then resumes picking up glass, praying it will quit. It persists. Annoyed and terrified, she tiptoes across the kitchen and lifts the receiver.

"Hello?" It is a whisper.

"Marta? I'm sorry. Were you sleeping?" The voice is unnaturally high, breathless.

She considers this. "No . . . no . . ." A pause, then, suspiciously, "Who is this?"

"*Alice*, silly. I figured you lost my number, so I'm calling you." A gorgeous, drunken giggle. "Listen, are you one half as bored as I am?"

"Alice . . ." Marta is undone. "Why weren't you at work?"

"I've saved enough sick time that I can have three-day weekends till March! I encourage you to do the same. It sure helps to put off the burnout a little longer. Now, what are your plans this evening? I'm going to get schnocked and giggle a lot, and maybe reveal some very personal things about myself. You won't want to miss it." She snorts between her sentences, Marta notes with some alarm.

"I don't know, Alice," she hears herself saying. "It's been a long day."

"It has," Alice agrees, her voice falling a few notches in pitch. "A really long day." She lets out a sigh, deflated. "Listen, would you like to come over? Or I could come there, if that's more convenient. I'll try not to be too annoying. I could just really use some company."

She sounds so suddenly defeated that Marta cannot refuse her without being cruel. It is not in her nature to be cruel, she insists to herself. She is truly sorry that the cat is cut and bleeding and hates her so much he will not let her tend to him, and profoundly sorry that Alice has no one better to turn to than a nervous recluse who can't even comfort a cat, much less look anyone in the eye. The ridiculous pathos of it makes her weepy, and she quickly mumbles directions so she can hang up and blow her nose. Alice sounds so miserably grateful Marta can barely keep the tremors out of her voice saying goodbye. *Pitiable creatures, all of us,* she thinks of herself, Alice, the cat. She cannot speak for the others but does not imagine they have it any better.

The cat emerges from under the sink and regards Marta quizzically as she splashes water on her face, over and over, snuffling wetly. He lifts and lowers his injured paw, licks at it gingerly. Marta kneels to the floor and extends a cautious hand, crooning to him softly. He allows one conciliatory stroke before retreating behind the pipes, watching her now, Marta imagines, with a shade less malice.

S HE
W AITS

H ale had a favorite blanket, as most children do, silky and frayed, and he would suck his thumb and daub softly at his upper lip with the unraveled fringe. An aesthete even then, a painter, a sensualist. The textures and delicate brushstrokes of his childhood. These are the things Hale's mother tells me, though I have already succumbed and no endearing stories about him are necessary. She shows me kindergarten photos of his fruit-plump face, but I have pressed my palms into the hollows of his cheeks, an old man's contours at twenty-five, only his lips still fleshy, his kisses fat. She pulls from between the pages of her photo album a length of ribbon that once measured the circumference of her pregnant belly, and I marvel how my fingers have caught on each rough nubbin of the spine that once was jelly in her womb. Hale's mother. I consider the plate tectonics of her son's head, pliant shifting puzzle pieces of skull fusing solid over his brain, now a mystery to her, murky folds into which I have nestled somehow. She is reluctant to part with her soft child's memory body, so she will share with me pictures, anecdotes, evidence of all their years before me. I am to call her Lois.

She is not intending to show me up, not really; we're new to each other, and there is little else to fill this awkward time. We have already toured the house, pausing only briefly to peer into Hale's old bedroom, freshly painted, trophyless and secretive. We have inspected the kitchen-nook-in-progress and finally settle there over cups of decaffeinated coffee at a table specked with sawdust and pink granules of insulation. Caffeine makes her heart race, she tells me, and to be clever and sweet, I want to tell her it is Hale that makes my heart race—though he doesn't. No reflection on him; I'm just not that way. My way of loving is to brood, and to fuss quietly over the small details. Plus I haven't taken very good care of her son, and so I won't try clever sweetness.

I am thirty-five. She—Lois—is forty-five. Hale, as I have mentioned, is twenty-five. I have not yet mentioned his drug rehab, and neither has she, though I took him and she's paying for it. That revelation took place over the phone two months ago, and we've spoken twice and only briefly since, for her to confirm his discharge day and for me to get directions to her house. I imagine she contains a welling bubble of grief and worry; this has made her careful in her dealings with me and vice versa. I say what seem like harmless things: how lovely the area, how expansively welcoming the house, how bracing the afternoon air, how sweet the bedraggled cat molting around my ankles, how incredibly sweet the pictures, the relics of her boy, how sweet he must have been, her fat soft babychild. Sweet cloying us both.

"Sweet, yes. Until around thirteen," she says. "Then he turned positively dour. Like most kids, I suppose." In these pictures he is gangly-ugly and scowling, caught unawares. Later he learned the grace to carry his long bones. His features stopped floundering around on his face and settled into a profound symmetry. Something—drugs, I'm assuming—focused his tensions, honed him. Then I found him, bones, beauty, and energy, chemical brittle. An art student, what else?

"You were his teacher," Lois says, more an observation than a question.

"Hale's metals class," I tell her. "I had no business teaching it. I'm mostly two-D design and illustration. But he wasn't my student anymore . . ." She's nodding intently, so I trail off before I say, "when we got together," or some other such general and inaccurate description of what he and I did.

She asks, "What did he—?" and stops. Presses her hand flat on the photo of Hale's thirteen-year-old scowl. Winces. She asked before, and I was vague, complicit.

"Use?" I say. "Coke, I think. I saw powders; I guess it was coke." It wasn't any one thing, though. I remember smelling ether in the stairwell, the snap of amyl nitrate, the stale reek of bong water. Once he punctured a can of refrigerant and took reckless huffs of freon. It lowered his voice to a rich bass, like the opposite of helium. That he tended to breathe his drugs might be the only constant. It's probably what started him on painting, those rich, sharp turpentine fumes searing his nostrils. Thinners and epoxies, shellacs. What will he do now? I wonder. How will he work?

"You don't . . . use?" she asks, one eyebrow cocked and skeptical, Hale's perpetual expression.

"No, not for a long time. Since my twenties." Silence. "That's why I didn't worry much about him at first, because people, you know, try things—"

"In their twenties," she finishes. "And you are . . . ?" She must know how old.

"Thirty," I lie.

If she does know, she lets it pass, thumbing pages. "He's leaving for college here, for the first time. He looked so much *healthier* then, much more color to him." Hale behind the wheel of his first car—now totaled. The sun gleams in his face and carefully wet-combed hair. He's waving, probably to Lois. He got mono his first semester and had to drop out, she explains. What he told me is that he just stopped going to classes after a month.

"He'll look healthier now, don't you think?" I say reassuringly, though I don't know what to think. I don't know what he'll look like or be like, because I haven't heard from him. I can't call him, and he hasn't called me since his first week in, when he said to me, "This is some place you left me at. Detox for dissolute singers. People say Ozzy Osbourne's been through here, and most of the Allman Brothers, and some bigtime soprano—but for her it didn't take."

"Shouldn't you call him Ozzy O.?" I asked, laughing. "Protect his anonymity? What didn't take?"

"The Program," he said, making it sound ominous. Then: "I may not call or write much, okay? They're keeping me real busy, and I want to stay focused."

I said, "Of course. We'll have plenty of time to talk when you get out." But then he really didn't call or write. It has left me with no footing.

"We should go," Lois says. I'm driving. Lois doesn't like to drive; something about her vision. She explains she *can* drive and does, but is relieved not to have to. This ought to shake Hale up good, the sight of his mother and his girlfriend come together to pick him up, the prospect of the three of us in my jittery little hatchback. To whose home? We haven't hashed over yet where it is we're taking him. I suppose he'll indicate his expectations, or we'll ask him and he'll choose. I find myself jerking the little car around corners a bit too fast.

I drove Hale the fourteen or so hours to the Minnesota rehab, all back roads because he'd dreaded the exposure of the interstate. "No smooth, vast expanse," he'd pleaded. "No multiple lanes." Among other things, he feared we'd get pulled over on the interstate. He claimed a smug midwestern patrolman would take in the sight of him, raw-eyed and trembling, and pat him down. Hale believed he could not survive the flesh-crawl of a pat-down. I couldn't leave his sight; he would squat beside me while I urinated in the brush. All that to get there, and he returns to me in a bus: public, official, hugely veering into the parking lot.

Lois lurches for him the moment he steps off, so I stand aside shyly while they embrace. She is much shorter; her face presses into his chest, and he grins over the top of her head at me. Winks. "Hiya, gals." Hale does have more color to him, but it's mostly more yellow around the fingers that clamp his cigarette. He's always smoked, but I'm thinking now it will be with a ferocity. A little extra weight softens his face in a pleasing way.

Lois pulls back to inspect him. "You look terrific. You need a haircut." Her eyes are moist.

It's my turn, and we grapple each other awkwardly, unsure of how to touch in front of his mother. I kiss his pliant cheek. "Are you ready?" I ask.

"I guess we'll find out," he says, nervous kidding.

On the drive back, Hale's knees press through the seat into the small of my back. His smoke wreathes my face. I want to take him home, to my home, pull off his slouchy rehab turtleneck and taste the salt on his skin. But at least for the next few days he owes his mother the reassurance of his company. It is now quite clear that this is what Lois expects.

She says, "We'll go to the grocery store. I don't know what you eat anymore."

"You know I eat anything," he answers gently.

"I guess they've been feeding you well," I offer.

"Oh yeah, good stuff. Healthy. A little fancy. Designs in the salad, that kind of thing." His knees pulse encoded messages to my back.

"Well, we're going to be slumming it, compared to that," Lois says. "We're sort of on a budget these days."

"You don't mean . . . not the cornflake meat loaf!" he shouts in mock horror. "Ma, do you want me to relapse?"

Lois twists in her seat to slap his leg. "Don't," she admonishes.

"Come on, Ma."

"We'll order something for tonight. Korean—you like that, right? We could get the barbecue."

"Whatever you want, Ma."

"No," she says tightly. "No. You tell me what you want to eat."

"Korean sounds good. Paige, you like Korean, right?" One knee prods.

"Absolutely." There's a hole yawning open in my stomach that could pass for hunger.

I linger through dinner, already forsaking my tiny budding friendship with Lois. If I truly wanted to foster good relations, I'd give her the gift of her son alone on his first night home, let her drink in his new wellness. Instead, the three of us sit around the table in the kitchen-nook-in-progress, gnawing the remaining cartilage off our barbecued short ribs.

"So," Lois keeps starting. "So," and then finally, "So what did you think of it? How are you now? I mean, really: How *are* you now?"

"Well, I could really use a drink," Hale quips, and we both glare at him.

"That is, if I wanted to die—which I don't," he finishes. "Really." That grin, sly, with no teeth showing.

"Because I would kill you," his mother says.

"So not even drinking now," I muse aloud.

"No; it's got to be everything."

"What about tobacco?" I ask as he lights a cigarette.

He sighs smoke. "It's all I got now."

"I can live with the smoking," says Lois, "for now. One thing at a time . . . or one day at a time, right?"

"Spoken like a twelve-stepper," says Hale.

"Well, I thought of going. This lady at work invited me to Al-Anon. I said I didn't think you were an alcoholic."

"I'm an addict, Mom. It's pretty much the same thing, at least from your standpoint. You should go."

"Well, I thought about it. I'm still thinking."

"You should go."

"I should have gone when you were still messed up. Except I didn't know you were messed up."

"I'm still messed up. You knew a little, didn't you?"

"You weren't even living here." An accusation of sorts, but her tone is subdued, I think for my benefit. I shouldn't be here. I should not.

"Mom, I was at it a long time before I ever left home." He stares at her intently. "And I think you knew that, even if you tried not to."

"Look, being around in the sixties doesn't make me some expert on drugs."

"It doesn't matter now, does it?" I pipe up, so helpful. Neither of them looks at me. "I mean, it's all in the open now, and that's the important thing. And Hale's better."

"Getting better," he corrects, reaching for my hand and giving it a promising squeeze. My insides quake with lust and discomfort. I want a shortcut through this thing between him and his mother, which has to reach some closure for the night if Hale and I are to be together.

I try a few more concluding remarks. "It's enough for now that you're back and feeling well. The past, who knew what, is not so important."

"Was it coke?" asks Lois.

"Among other things," he replies.

"Well, I did think coke, maybe. Though I can't imagine how you afforded it."

"I had ways," he offers vaguely. "You do what it takes." His gaze drops, and he resumes picking at his rice.

Not even I know what he means; he seems to be referring to things darker than I ever saw. Questions to be answered later, I suppose. For me right now, it seems as if everything could be resolved in one fell swoop of lovemaking, or forgiven in the blessed aftermath.

"I have a lot of amends to make," he says to both of us, finally. "A lot."

"You don't have to make them all tonight," I say helplessly.

"No," Lois agrees.

"No," Hale echoes, "but I do need to get started on this thing. There's this guy in town I need to call. They gave me his number so I could get ahold of him about meetings and stuff."

"Your sponsor?" Lois asks.

"He could turn out to be, I suppose. Or he could hook me up with one."

"So call him," I say, betrayed. "You've been here, what, an hour? Don't let another minute go by."

Lois shoots me a brief, alarmed glance, then settles her attention back gently to her son. It's so expansive and benign, her gaze, taking all of him in. Her righteous concern. My greed and impatience shames me, but I'm not his mother, don't want to be.

"Hey," he says with that new gentleness, stroking my hand. "Hey."

"Hey what." Sullen isn't a good idea tonight, but I can't help it.

"Hey, I don't have to call him tonight. Just soon. Tomorrow."

"You learned some things in there, I gather," Lois interjects smoothly, relieving me of having to make another sulky response.

"Yeah, you could say that." Hale laughs. "It'd be a major understatement, but you could say it. My second week in . . . We had all these rules, see? You couldn't break them, and you had to tell if you saw somebody else breaking them, or you'd be in as much shit. They made it sound like somehow it would come out that you'd known and done nothing, that probably the caught person would even offer you up."

He stops to consider this. Then, "Some of that seems like just so much bullshit from here, and I'm not even clear now on what they held over us as punishment. You'd get booted out, I suppose; you'd just fail at rehab. A few people crapped out while I was there, and after they were gone, for a day it was like they'd died, then after that like they'd never even been there. You basically forgot all about them, except you just didn't want to follow in their tracks."

Lois and I are silent. Hale's cigarette has gone out, and he lights a fresh one, pulls hard on it.

"Anyway, one of the rules had to do with sexual contact— basically to forget about it. No relationships that might turn into sexual, either. There were women in our groups and everything; it was important to hear from everybody, you know, get insights on different people's addictions and how they're working through them. But if they saw people pairing up, they'd get them separated fast. And sleeping arrangements were very separate, a guys' wing and a girls' wing, locked and patrolled to a certain extent. They didn't shine a light in your bunk or anything, but somebody walked the halls at night. If you got up to go to the bathroom, somebody was like, Hey, man, what's up? Real friendly and concerned but also to let you know not to be trying to get away with anything in the bath-room in the middle of the night.

"I shared a room with these two other guys—it was generally three or four to a room—and early on I'm just pull-ing that fidgety kind of doze, because I'm still not used to the schedule there or to sharing a room like that. My room-mates started right around the same time as me, and they were doing okay, sort of dazed like I was but going along with it all, I thought. I'm just kind of snoozing alert, and I hear these, I don't know, *wet* sounds. So I just glance over without turning my head much, and their bodies are kind of lumped together on one bed, one's all the way under the blanket."

Lois's face is so blank and set I can't read it. But tight-seeming, teeth clamped against this.

"I'm like, damn, because it's none of my business and to each his own, and if I hadn't been such a nervous sleeper, I'd never even have known what was going on. I kind of coughed and thrashed around like I was still asleep and they got quiet, and in a little while I heard one creep back to his bed. I didn't say anything, but in a couple of days, Frank was out of there. I don't know if that was why, but I was scared to death they somehow found out I knew and hadn't told, and that I would be sent home. The other guy didn't make it, either, I can't remember his name.

"Not long after that, a girl offered me some powder, and I narced on her almost immediately. I'm not even sure now if she was for real or just some kind of a test for me. But everybody seemed real pleased with me, and I was seriously into it after that. I didn't want *anybody* getting in the way of my recovery."

Anybody includes me, I realize.

Lois rises, starts gathering plates. "Coffee?" she offers.

"No, thanks," I say. "I should probably go." But I don't move. I look to Hale for some sign of what to do. He strokes my hand, but there are no more messages like back in the car, which I'm thinking now were just his long legs restless and pistoning from travel. He smokes thoughtfully, keeps stroking my hand. I get up, finally, and feel no resistance to my leaving.

Lois is at the sink, letting the water run and foam over dishes. "Good to finally meet you in person," I tell her, ready to shake hands or something, but she doesn't turn around. I pat her shoulder uncertainly.

She turns off the water, slowly wipes her hands on her pants. "Yes. Same here. Thanks for driving—for all your driving. Thanks for looking after him."

"Well, I don't know about that," I'm saying, as she turns around and surprises me with a hard pulse of a hug, fiercely sincere and abrupt.

"You'll come back?" she asks.

"Of course," I manage.

Hale walks me out to my car, and I wrap my arm around his waist, holding on. I stop to embrace him, and his arms envelop me, but he continues to walk me to the car, his knees nudging mine to keep me moving. He leans me against the car door and kisses me deep, like a daydream of kissing. His tongue sweeps mine, darts along my teeth and palate, slick and hungry, and for a moment I am collapsing in the sweetness.

I push him away. "I missed you," I accuse.

"Well, I missed *you*." He laughs, pulling me back.

"So what happens now? Do you stay here, do you come home with me?"

"You know I want to be with you . . ." he begins.

"But."

"It's just tonight. I don't know. My mom . . ."

"Yes, yes, I realize, I know. Your mom."

"Maybe I can come later," he offers. "Will you be awake?" His fingers rake my scalp.

"Like I can sleep," I murmur into his shoulder and bite down gently.

"I'll try," he says, and I know that he will, but it isn't enough. I lock my hands around his head and draw his face back to seal mine. I don't want to breathe, don't need air. I just want to submerge, languish at the dark bottom of this sea, the deep-water crush, but instead I feel myself surfacing, bobbing back to the top like a cork. For now it's all right, though, this buoyancy, this floating. It feels a little like optimism.

It has been only two weeks now, and it's understandable, it's well within reason—it is in fact the only *sensible* thing that Hale should still be at his mother's house. That we should all get our bearings and be methodical about it. That nothing will resume in quite the same way, and that this is a good thing. But what I don't see the sense of is this nightly drama of will he or won't he come over. I try to prepare for either eventuality. It is important in the beginning, he tells me, for him to get to a meeting every day, and evenings are the best time for him to go. Hale's lapse from the strict rehab schedule has been immediate and extreme. He sleeps throughout the day, and Lois has been kind when I've called, but firm; she will not wake him, will not interfere. He's bleary-eyed and pacing the kitchen by five-thirty or six, digging up something for his breakfast, her supper. It's rightfully their time, and I'm steering clear. But after that is the meeting, and after that, me. If the conditions are right. If the planets are properly aligned. He's often wired after the meeting's infusion of coffee and cigarettes and confessions, and so sometimes it's best for him to continue this into the night with his sponsor. I am to assume this has happened if I don't hear from him.

Just before midnight, I give up on Hale officially and head out. I have applied a deep-red lip liner to fashion my mouth into a shapely gash, and bruisy smudges of kohl encircle my eyes. I have achieved that wrecked look so appealing in the murky light of the bars. It isn't subtlety, but it could be art: the resonant tap of my hard, narrow shoes, the cloud of musk that precedes me like a rumor, my crunchy red cap of hair. "Guess how old I am," I will challenge someone who will err on the side of youth, because I am on the smooth, compact end of thirty-five; I am small, with dainty hands and feet to match, pert in all the good places. I sometimes get carded at the doors in spite of my makeup, or maybe because of it; it looks like I could be trying too hard.

Tonight I'm only going to Malphie's, where the bartender knows me and keeps an eye out. I'm not looking for revenge or trouble. It's just part of an old ritual, and even incomplete, it soothes. I remember Malphie's at its best going on ten years ago, when it was still boasting grand opening streamers and tropical drink specials. I was a grad student playing at being married then, stenciling designs on thrift store chairs for our kitchen. My husband and I used to come here to drink gimlets and play shuffleboard.

I called him my husband though he never was, legally speaking. It was a decision we'd made so as not to complicate our student loan paperwork, which had been coming along nicely thus far. We both agreed there was no reason to interfere with the original formulas; they had somehow caused our checks to be dispensed regularly, so we shied from deviation. Still, our commitment would be private and earnest and every bit as binding, we agreed in near-spousal fashion. Such thrift and regularity in those days, our lovemaking precise as clock-work, our days calibrated to spool out the appropriate lengths of work, studies, household labors, private time, our money carefully budgeted to allow for movies and weekend cocktails at Malphie's. So fair, so even-keel, it famined us. I got hungry for love's inconsistencies, lumpy as batter.

I worked myself loose, or fell out of sync, something. I started getting serious about art but mostly about makeup and got this idea that I would start doing makeup—not cosmetic-counter, accentuate-the-positive nonsense, but exaggerations, masklike caricatures superimposed over the face. Nothing ever came of it except a prototype of my bar face, a little more lop-sidedly cruel than the version I'm wearing now. That and a brief "collaboration" with a photography student, which has-tened the breakup of my not-really marriage. He wasn't con-tent just to photograph my face, and I wasn't content at that, either. I still have the negatives.

"Guess how old I am," I challenge the bartender, who sets a gimlet before me without my having to ask, my little bonus for the years and money spent.

He grins, an old acquaintance. "I know better."

"That's because *you're* old enough to know better," I retort, my mouth tangy with lime juice. "But how old am I?"

"You're only as old as you feel," he says, a friendly evasion.

"Hell, then I must be about a hundred."

He waves my proffered bills away. "You better have this one on the house, then." He doesn't linger for my thank-you.

I nurse the gimlet, realizing I have only these four dollars and that at least one should go as a tip. That's what happens when you don't budget; you stay sober. Maybe Hale should have tried that, but really that's a weak supposition, good only as long as you feel like staying sober. If I wanted more to drink, I could get it. The question is, how much do I want another drink? Enough to flirt a little? It seems like bad luck to think like this now that Hale's back. A bit of a betrayal, perhaps, for me to come here and drink when Hale can't anymore, but all the waiting is catching up with me. I can't help but think I wouldn't even be here if he were truly back. His visits are so late-night ethereal, I often wonder the next morning if I didn't dream them. The daylight, his absence, only these are solid. And I'll have to keep on waiting while he sorts things out, waiting for him to grow up and catch up, for him to work his twelve-step deal or lay it aside, finish college and formulate some life plan—much as I did, only to discard it in favor of a more comfortable intimacy, which will then begin to wear on him. I'm not sure that I have time to wait for him to do even half the things I did, though I scrounge for more time like change hidden in my purse.

I leave a dollar for the bartender and wave goodnight to him as I head out, smiling at the appreciative murmurs from the men clustered at the TV end of the bar. "Oh, *please* don't go, pretty baby!" one of them wails as I pass, and I am buoyed by the plaintiveness of it. That and my trace of a vodka buzz almost pulls me back toward them, but no, I can't stay. Back at my apartment, the phone must be ringing; I am willing it to ring with each step, readying it to begin just as I am ascending the stairs. Let him wonder: Is she sleeping? Could she possibly sleep? Or is she gone? And just as the tendrils of anxiety are working their way into him, I will pick up the phone, a bit breathy and distracted, which I won't explain.

I don't know how I got in so deep. It's not that I have any special weakness for talent or potential; as a sometimes teacher, I see a lot of that. And anyway, Hale's sloppy verdigris abstractions earned him a C in my metals class. But when he asked if he could draw me, I was flattered enough to say yes. I liked his eyes to flicker from me to his image of me, liked to hear the rasp of his charcoals like a sexy whisper. I liked to see what it was he made of me. I couldn't help but notice how he took everything further than his friends: lived hard, slept hard or not at all. Hale seemed gorgeously bent on destruction, his energy shimmering off in my arms, my arms bringing rest.

He would take whatever someone offered him and then ask what it was. One time he snorted goddamn animal tranquilizer; not PCP, exactly, but some white powder along those lines, filched from somebody's veterinarian father. I wasn't there when he did it, but his friends told me he'd been drinking too. Most of them were doing mushrooms, just grooving along peaceably, then Hale put his head down between his legs and moaned for somebody to call me, have me come get him, but nobody was ready to deal with a phone call just then. By the time someone was, Hale was on the floor, gray-faced, his eyes lolling around in his head. Some kind of seizure, his friends figured.

One of them called me. "We can't handle this," he explained. "We need somebody straight to take a look at him."

"Call an ambulance," I insisted, but he put the phone to Hale's face so I could hear that he was still breathing and begged me just to come and see first.

"We could get in a lot of trouble," he pleaded. "Just please be cool and check it out first." They all thought I was cool, you see, and I prided myself on that. And it wasn't the first time I'd been summoned to come get Hale, though it was a sort of milestone in that it was my first inkling of real danger. We hadn't been together quite six months, but it clinched things for me.

When I got there, Hale was sitting up. He smiled at me weakly but very much alive. "Am I glad to see *you*," he managed. Love flooded me like relief, or maybe it was the other way around. I brought him back to my apartment, where he kept on for four more unsteady months until he asked me to take him to the rehab center. I was fully in support of it except for his having to move out, a misgiving I have graciously kept to myself.

My conjuring has worked for once—the phone is ringing as I get in. I race to grab it before it stops.

"Paige? Paige, I'm sorry to call so late." It's Lois. "Did Hale make it over there, by any chance?"

"No. Did he say he was heading this way? I've been out." I'm ashamed of the gimlet on my breath, as if she could detect it.

"He said if it got too late he'd go to your house. I'm such a light sleeper, he said he didn't want to wake me."

"Where did he say he was going?"

"With his old friends, his so-called friends," Lois wails. "I just didn't think he ought to go off with them so soon. But they kept calling and finally showed up, saying they'd take him out for *coffee*. What could I say? He's known them since high school. I should have insisted he stay here, but what could I say?"

"I don't know. He's got to decide, I guess."

"Exactly! And the thing is," Lois continues, "I didn't really feel that he wanted to go with them. I felt like maybe he hoped I would insist, but he's got to do that for himself. He has to set the rules. I was hoping he'd be there with you by now."

"He'll show up soon, I bet," I say. "I'll call you." The old worry is pulsing through me again, insistent as lust.

She's quiet for a few seconds. Then, "No, I don't want you to do that. I don't want things this way, me checking up on him like this."

"It's just for your peace of mind tonight," I say. "It's perfectly understandable."

"No, just call me in the morning, if you would. Maybe we can all meet for breakfast. I want to do this right."

"Me too," I tell her, thinking breakfast with Hale doesn't seem likely.

"And if he doesn't show, then *we'll* have breakfast. I mean, if you want."

"That sounds good," I say. "Why don't you try to get some sleep."

"I'm going to try really hard," she insists. "You try too."

I promise her I will, but I mean it about as much as I think she does, huddled in her half-finished kitchen nook, sipping decaf, waiting for dawn. Though I don't have a mother's patience, stoic and infinite, I think I can wait at least that long.

State

of

Repair

"Alma has a cyst but it's benign," says the brother who calls intermittently to announce the latest in his life of close calls and near misses. Second in line for the job; his next-door neighbor's house burgled; an inch higher, and the impact would have paralyzed him. He is all sprains and no broken bones. What would he do, Nell wonders, if something of note actually happened to him? He seems so satisfied with mere proximity.

But what has *she* done, really? Nell was absent from her own "event," the only really exciting and near-tragic thing that happened to her. She'd been angry at Milt for another remark, made cruelly and quiet, under his breath. She recognized the tone—wry indictment of her, the marriage—and she left the house when she felt the rage unfurling in her belly. Best to remove herself from the situation until it worked itself out of her. Otherwise, more things would be said, horrible things, difficult to retract later. Nell would murmur them under her breath just out of earshot.

It seemed like the right thing to do, slipping silently out, keys crunched in her fist. Nell drove intently away, savoring the self-control used to not accelerate through the streets of her neighborhood. She felt magnanimous, willing to spare the children who might veer innocently off the curb and into her path.

Away from Milt, Nell knows she acts reasonably, with concern for the welfare of others. No one but Milt sees the way she can shake and keen with anger. Her brother, maybe, but years ago, long forgotten. She mostly serves him as an appreciative whew! on the other end of the line when he calls, even now, though he doesn't ask how they are doing in their scorched, stinking house, which they still aren't sleeping in. For him, it is a close call to tell to others, Nell reasons: the sister visited by tragedy.

"Twenty more laid off in engineering . . ." the brother says. "Our yard boy has heel spurs. He won the lottery, though. . . ." Nell sees him, slender and pockmarked, tiptoeing through crabgrass, uprooting dandelions with a pearl-handled ebony cane. It is an oddly erotic vision, and Nell mumbles that she really, really must go. Time for the roof man to come and make an estimate. She slips the phone gently back into its cradle.

She peers out the kitchen window to see if her words have conjured him, but sees only the boys skateboarding resolutely up and down her block, as if nothing has happened. One is the culprit, Nell is sure. Who else but these summer-drunk boys would shoot a bottle rocket through her attic window? In the days surrounding the fourth of July, they had been in possession of a small arsenal and had declared war on the neighborhood: an explosion poised behind every shrub, or the billowing blue smoke of a stink bomb. It is difficult for Nell to distinguish between them in their like uniforms of loose, floppy clothes and hair swinging forward to obscure the face. Only the close-cropped backs of their heads bare the baby curve of skull, of slender white neck, naked and vulnerable.

The attic with its echoey-raftered church angles was to have been her place of solace. Milt spoke of renovating to give the house an upstairs guest bedroom/office spot, but Nell refused. She felt she needed loose, crumbly insulation and dusky trunks brimming with old letters and winter clothes. "Give me something to haunt," she'd said. She hadn't even wanted this house until she stood on the naked planks of the attic floor and peered out the dingy half-moon window. The crime is against her.

Nell gathers up her gardening tools, the most rusty and wicked of the lot; her dauntless weeding will shame the boys. But as she strides outside, a truck swerves into her driveway with a piquant squeal of brakes. Its sudden brute appearance, black and cantankerous, startles the boys, scattering them to the far corners of the neighborhood.

The driver steps out and Nell locks onto his boots, made of gleamy reptile skin. They are luminous, magnificent; they delight Nell—she wants to see her naked body reflected in them. But he can't possibly fix her roof in those boots, Nell thinks, imagining the hot tar dribbling all over, obscuring her image.

"You are here for the estimate," she confirms. "That's all."

"Oh yes, ma'am. Just need to check the damage. Can't do any work until we've assessed the situation." He tilts his head back, surveys the upper portion of the house through a squint. He is older, though not old. Tanned and craggy in the way that men in Milt's family do not get. They are pale and argyled; they putter around competently but hire out for the big jobs like roofs, plumbing, projects requiring cement. They grow putty-soft with age.

The roof man is lean; he tilts an aluminum ladder against the side of the house and scales it with spider swiftness. He is a man accustomed to slants. Gripping the chimney with one hand, he folds back the tarp, gently, as if waking a child. He peels back shingles, prods areas for softness. He leans in close and sniffs.

"Need to look in that attic now," he calls down to Nell, descending the ladder. He pauses to pull away the plastic and uses the heel of his boot to clear the jagged line of glass from the window. He slips inside.

When the roof man emerges, he will want more information, Nell thinks. It was a small attic fire, smothered within an hour of detection. There was talk of wiring and joists, but Nell has the impression the impact on these things wasn't great. The roof man should be able to take care of it all. "Skilled in Carpentry," his card promised, among other things. If he cannot, friends and family will be consulted. There will be recommendations and inquiries, more estimates made. The house will be repaired, regardless. The process has already been set in motion.

Still, Nell hopes the roof man is able to do it all. The event will then come full circle, a series of linked incidents deeply infused with meaning. This is what she knows: As the bottle rocket sailed through the open half-moon window and made a slow, spreading circle of ash, she was on her angry drive. As it fed on her dry, papery things, she strolled through the antiques mall—*Over 90 Booths! Filled with Reminiscence!* Bionic Woman lunch boxes and bright fondue pots, relics of her adolescence—flameproof mementos; the irony is not lost on Nell. Then the fire latched onto things that made acrid smoke and hot plastic smells, alerting Milt, who promptly dialed 911. Nell feels certain it was at this very moment that she plucked the roof man's card from the bulletin board at the mall's exit, seemingly by accident. It was stuck with the same pushpin as the quiltmaker's card she'd been reaching for, so she pocketed them both.

"My sister," her brother would tell people, "had a psychic episode connected to the tragedy."

Nell told Milt that her boss had referred the roof man to them, but if it works out, she will own up to this bit of magic.

Nell had returned home from the antiques mall, calm and lucid, to find Milt, the fire chief, and most of the neighbors standing in the yard, heads tilted back to watch the upper half of the house finish its slow, dwindling smolder. She arrived only in time for the aftermath of paperwork, a small catastrophe in itself. Still, the half-moon window was broken out, the gray roof had turned melty soot-black in patches. Smoke hung thick and cloying inside, even downstairs, and the house might not be habitable for days, the fire chief had said, penciling abbreviated expert observations onto his clipboard. Nell had fingered the slick card in her pocket.

Milt had taken out his laptop computer, their wedding album, and the wicker cat carrier, Bones yowling in protest within. The cat crackled at her touch, but Nell couldn't stop embracing him. To Milt she said, "What about the clothes?" and noted the almost imperceptible tight pulse at his jawline. A whole trunk of winter clothes, though! She knows *she* would have thought of it.

They spend their nights at his parents' house, pressed together on the twin bed in his old room, its walls still thick with pennants and a rock band collage.

"I thought you were up there, at first," Milt murmured to her there that first night, his cheek adhered to her neck with sweat. "I heard sounds, and then that hot plastic smell . . . and I thought for a minute you might be up there." A brief sob puffed out of him, and Nell clutched him fiercely, exultant. Though she is unsure now whether he was telling her he was afraid she was caught in the fire or thought that she had set the fire. He has assumed a hand-patting attentiveness to Nell that could mean either.

"Do you mind hanging around for the estimate?" he asked Nell this morning, driving her to the house to drop her there on his way to work. "I can take a sick day if you don't want to be alone," but Nell told him no, no, to go ahead on. This was nothing. This she could do. Milt was earnest and pandering, and Nell got a twinge she still hasn't figured out.

Nell decides she prefers to be thought capable of setting fires. How like her to torch the place and then whine placatingly, "I just wanted something to *happen!*" In college, when she and Milt had dated long enough for him to sink into complacency, Nell countered by sleeping with his roommate. ("My sister is embroiled in a ménage à trois," her brother, then a bookish junior, bragged to his chem lab partner.) Not two weeks after, Milt proposed. It's the little jolts, Nell thinks, that cement their relationship.

Nell hears an indoor-muffled great thud and clattering, runs in to find the roof man sprawled in the hallway, powdered white with plaster. It appears he has tried to climb down from the attic via the rickety fold-out ladder steps, and the ceiling around the opening has collapsed. For a moment he is clenched, gasping and prone, but he recovers enough at Nell's appearance to sit up, untangle his thin legs from the rungs, and ask for something cold to drink.

Nell brings him a glass of iced tea, kneels in the rubble beside him. "I got your card off a bulletin board the day of the fire. *During* the fire," she adds meaningfully. "I didn't even know yet that I was looking for you." Nell wills him to have no injuries, to have good news for her. This must all be part of the groundbreaking, the christening of what's to be sounder shelter. She drizzles a bit of the tea on the floor. Let the old burned and rotting beams give; we'll put more and better in. Destruction begins repair, sets it in motion. It moved forward inevitably from the purchase of cheap explosives en masse just over the state line, every nearby match for days a tiny embryo. Smoke issuing from her husband's mouth, the red glow knotting her belly. Her finger turns red and scaly beneath the wedding ring, burns until she twists it off, burns until she slips it back on, burns. Flames glossing the roof. Already the process was under way.

Nell rises, thinking she'll get a broom, she'll bring this man a damp towel to wipe the ghost powder away. She'll clean his boots. But she stands there.

The roof man tips back the tea too quickly and coughs. Rivulets stream down the corners of his mouth, etching flesh lines through the white. The chin, delineated, becomes a separate piece that will wobble obliging puppet answers.

Listen to me, he will say. It's hardly more than a patch job. A few things need replacing, but she's good and solid. It won't cost much. It won't take long. I'll do it all myself. Keep that tarp on for rain, but you can come back and live here while I fix it.

She waits for this. He looks indecisive or possibly just dazed. A word, she thinks. Just give me a word. It can't be that far gone.

"It's not bad, is it?" Nell prompts. Yes, no?

The roof man broods beneath her gaze. He lifts up slightly, massages his rump. He nudges a ragged slab of debris with the pointed toe of his boot, flips it to reveal the underbelly, where fire fused plank floor to ceiling and blackened it to brittle, gleaming charcoal.

Meals and
Between Meals

Helena is the visitor, friend, not relation, fat, pink, and wreathed in a brittle yellow cloud of hair. Mag is the inmate, *her* inmate, sinewy lean, arms scribbled with blurry tattoos. Beneath the picnic tablecloth in a far corner of the courtyard, she clasps his mottled turkey-neck penis. One of his forearms extends up into her dress, where his fingers squeeze an expanse of her thigh. Her girth engulfs them both, helps obscure the errant hands from view. The tight armholes of Helena's dress still welt her, but her belly is less intent against the seams than before; she is reducing slowly, out of love. His mother has come earlier in the day, baleful, to slip him a twenty, which Mag folds into a flat tablet and slides between lip and gum. His mother is afraid not to; he tells her it's for his protection. "Ma," he says, "they'll kill me." "Should let you die," she says, but has already handed it over.

Helena and Mag have two hours together on Sunday afternoons. Helena brings him cigarettes and paperbacks and rolls of summer sausage. She writes his name all over the packages in red marker and checks them in with the guard. Because today is a picnic day, Helena has been permitted to carry in a bucket of fried chicken and slaw. Its crisp, oily presence continues to tempt her; the struggle to resist eating a wing or leg in the car on the way over was epic in the emotions it produced. Her diet club says to Be Here Now, meaning never to eat when distracted, while driving or watching TV or talking on the phone; you lose track and are pretty soon at the bottom of the bag of chips or the cookie jar. Let it be a singular action that you experience fully—you will be satisfied with less food, they say.

Helena tries to apply this philosophy to Mag's hand job, but it is too much of an obligatory routine. She feels an awed romantic weepy love for Mag, but no desire. She still believes herself too fat for desire, a self-esteem issue they are hammering out at the diet club. Mag's grip on her thigh is as shaming an appraisal as the clamp they use to gauge her body-fat percentage each month.

Helena toggles Mag's penis with renewed intent, but it slowly withers in her hand. She feels contrite because her enthusiasm was insincere. Mag just shrugs and tucks it back in his pants; the whims of the body don't seem to trouble him much. He reaches for the bucket of chicken and takes one languid bite from a drumstick. Mag likes to bite the choicest hunks out of a breast or leg piece, then set it aside and go on to the next. Helena pulls the seal off her bowl of salad and eats with her fingers, cucumbers first, then carrots, tomato, and finally lettuce, focusing hard on enjoying the moment, on being here now: *This is good food, good for you, crunchy and full of vitamins, this is the food to give a body you love—so why do you bring Mag junk? Because he likes it, because he is lean and knobby with bones, because he can eat and eat and eat and only be lean and knobby with bones.*

The salad is like eating paper, like eating nothing. Helena carefully peels a chicken breast, blots the excess grease from her fingers with a napkin, and devours the lean white meat. She hesitates only a moment more before thrusting the glistening wad of skin in her mouth, which finally comes alive with juices.

Mag says, "I want you to talk to Mr. Williams about me."

"I have," Helena insists. "I've tried. He won't call me back anymore." Mr. Williams runs an office-cleaning operation and has been known to hire ex-convicts. Mag needs a sponsor to be eligible for home passes and, eventually, work release. They won't let Helena be the sponsor; they know she's his girlfriend, and they know she can't provide him with employment.

She could, however, provide him with a place to live when he gets out, if his mother won't. Mag has talked wistfully about sleeping late at Helena's house, leaving the doors and windows wide open, and watching whatever he chooses on television—maybe having a beer or two when he wants one. "But not too many," Mag has assured her. "You know where that gets me!" though Helena doesn't know, really. In prison, she guesses. "My needs are few, baby," he has told her, and they do seem dwarfed by the swollen expanse of their love. But Mr. Williams isn't returning Helena's calls, and she doesn't know what she can do about that.

"Did you tell him to ask Glenn about me?" Mag asks.

"I told him. But he says Glenn isn't a good reference." It seems that Glenn, in flagrant violation of his parole, blew the gaskets on a company van driving it to Atlantic City, where he hocked the vacuum cleaners for money to play blackjack and to slip into the G-strings of exotic dancers. "Glenn is a thieving asshole," is what Mr. Williams told Helena before he hung up with finality.

"Yeah, because the parole thing. But his word's good. Tell him that," Mag insists.

Helena, with tact: "Mag, honey, even if that's true, I don't think Mr. Williams is going to be impressed."

"Glenn knows how to read a man. It's what kept him alive in here." Mag's eyes glass over with tears, and his voice trebles shrilly. "He said he would help me, since he saw I had potential." His fist slams the table. "He promised!"

"We'll find somebody to do it, Magpie," Helena assures, clamping him in a squeeze. Mag has told her people freeze at the age they were when they first got locked up, which would make him something like thirteen if you count juvenile detention, and Helena does. Mag wriggles out of her grip, irritated, and reaches again for the chicken. Chastened, Helena picks at the slaw, eating one shred of cabbage at a time. She wonders how long a walk will undo the chicken skin she has eaten. She decides to walk briskly to her diet club meeting and back, and this earns her a wing, skin and all. She grinds the soft bone tips in her molars, sucks at the marrow, determined to finish off even the evidence, but Mag has stopped eating to stare at her in fascination. She spits wing debris into her napkin.

Clint strolls over with his instant camera. "Looking good in that dress," he says, grinning hopefully at Helena. "How about it?" Helena gives him two dollars, and he snaps their picture. A shiny white square projects from the camera, and they all watch the image coalesce on its surface: Mag with his narrow boy grin, the unlit cigarette he's suddenly thrust between his lips jutting up; Helena leaning in to rest her massive hairdo on his shoulder, her shiny doubled chin making her look like the one responsible for the wealth of chicken remains strewn on the table in front of them, she thinks, then quickly recants: *Self-love, not self-loathe.* All around them, bright umbrellas tilt over other picnic tables, holding couples and families. They could almost be at the park, only the men all wear slate-gray work shirts, and barbed wire spirals across the top of the high fence backdrop.

"Good composition," Clint observes, lingering over the picture. "You two look real nice."

"Have some chicken," Mag offers expansively, but only the liver and gizzard are left intact. Clint shakes the bucket, and the dry fried innards rattle like seeds in a gourd. Mag sniggers.

"You talk to Patty much?" Clint asks Helena. "She seeing anybody?" Clint's wife, Patty, is Helena's cousin. Helena used to come with her to visit Clint, which is how she met Mag. Patty stopped coming when she filed for divorce, but by then Mag had added Helena to his own visitor list.

"I'm not getting into it with you," Helena warns him gently.

"Getting into what?" Clint asks, all innocence.

Helena sighs. "No."

"No, what? You don't see her?"

"No, I'm not getting into it with you."

"Helena, you got to give me something . . . ," he begins, then appears to give up. "All right, all right. I see how it is. Well. You lovebirds have yourself a nice afternoon." Clint turns and walks away, still talking. "Yes indeed, a nice afternoon." He has a strangely gentle anger, which puzzles Helena. She doesn't think she has ever even heard Clint curse, while Mag is quick to lash out at the smallest provocation.

"Don't go away mad," Mag hollers after him. He studies the photo. "Baby, show this to Mr. Williams, so he can tell I'm okay. He can see for himself."

"Mag, honey—"

"Baby, just show it to anybody, all right? You got to help me out here." Mag pokes his lips out, pouty, then lowers his face into his hands. He shudders for a minute as if racked with sobs, then spreads his fingers and glares through them at Helena. He sticks his tongue out between his hands, retracts it, and growls, then giggles.

"Magpie, you so silly," Helena croons. Mag snatches her hand suddenly and pulls it into his lap, thrusts against it. "Baby, you . . . got . . . to help . . . me . . . out." Her forearm is nearly as thick as his thigh, Helena notes, but for the first time she sees cords of tendons flexing in her wrist and blue ghost traces of vein pressing closer to the skin when she grasps him in her fist.

"You *weren't* eating fried chicken!" Patty whispers incredulously.

"Just the white meat. Just the one." Helena lies without much hesitation, since she has held up one half of her bargain and walked to the diet club. "Mostly I had salad." She tucks the incriminating photo back in her purse. Patty is down to a size ten, and her cheeks are saggy pouches, half deflated. Her smile helps prop them back up only slightly. Her eyes are wider and more expressive, though, the way Helena remembers from when they were girls. Patty's melancholy streak has been long hidden behind doughy squints that gave her eyes a deceptively twinkling, Santa-jolly effect. As the weight comes off, gravity pulls at the corners of her mouth and eyes. Many of the successful dieters Helena has seen here have the same drawn look, but she thinks it lends them a sweet bloodhound appeal, beseeching and mournful.

The diet club takes up three storefronts in an otherwise abandoned shopping center. One is the Sustenance Shoppe, where Helena and Patty meet early to choose freeze-dried entrees for the coming week. The packets sport pictures of colorful, sensually shaped food heaped on fine china, but the actual choices are mostly variations on soup and pudding. Patty chooses fat-free instant polenta, three-bean vegetarian chili, and a hot cereal called FibreGrain Medley, "a natural laxative." Helena recalls the sheen of Velveeta on salty nachos at the prison canteen and tries to console herself with a pouch of (Good As) Guacamole, though she knows it will be altogether the wrong color of green. There have been allegations of spleen loss among former diet club members, so lately they've also been touting vitamin supplements. Patty dismisses the spleen as dead weight, "useless as tonsils," but Helena buys a bottle of FemForm with extra iron and folic acid. She likes to suck the glossy pink pills like candy.

They pay for their supplies and pass through to the next room to join the weigh-in line leading to a giant scale. An assistant, firm in the leotard and tights beneath her lab coat, stands by, recording the numbers.

"Clint's asking about you," Helena tells Patty.

"I figured. I got three hang-up calls this afternoon. What did you tell him?"

"You know I don't tell him anything."

Patty sighs with irritation, then turns away and scans the line, looking for other people she knows. She waves at a couple of friends and chats with the girl behind them, expressing a protracted admiration for her shoes, denim ballet slippers set with rhinestones.

When she is satisfied Helena has felt the full force of her disapproval, Patty turns back to face her. "Helena, you have to give him a little something to tide him over, or else I get those hang-up calls."

"I thought when I told him stuff you got hang-up calls."

"I do, but they're friendlier. He hangs up gently instead of slamming it in my ear." Patty used to change her number, but she felt she needed to give it to the prison so she could be reached in some emergency, like Clint having a heart attack or busting loose. Always he manages to get it again, so she has stopped bothering to change it.

Helena imagines poor Clint spending his afternoon recreational time changing the two dollars she paid him for the photo into quarters and feeding them into the pay phone one by one, just to hang up on his ex-wife. "It's not like he's meeting so many women," she observes sympathetically.

Patty scrunches her face. It was, after all, the fat, no-self-esteem Patty who married Clint in the first place, knowing he was a mediocre photographer and a worse thief. Size-ten-and-counting-down Patty wears forty-eight-dollar moisturizer and slinky velvet pants and dates a raisin-skinned man Helena calls the Tycoon because of his gleaming, blood-colored Cadillac. Patty will soon have operations to tighten her droopy cheeks and perk up her boobs, an early Christmas present from the Tycoon, who could use a little tightening himself.

This Patty says, "Hell, Mag met *you*, didn't he? Don't tell me Clint can't meet any women. There's plenty of women going over there just to slobber all over some fool criminal."

Helena reminds Patty quietly, "I only started going because you asked me."

"I know it, sweetie. I don't mean you. But you know what I'm talking about. Those women who go there and write to them and stuff. They don't set their sights so high."

We are those women! Helena wants to shout, but only she is anymore. As they approach the scale, anxiety balloons her. Her dress becomes a flimsy husk, barely able to contain her swollen spheres of breasts and belly and buttocks. Will she burst? She tests her buttons with plump, tight fingers, throttled by her rings, but really she is smaller, the scale confirms.

She finds the new slack in her dress, plucks at it, and feels herself recede.

Ten glasses of water a day will flush out the toxins and thwart hunger, which is often merely thirst in disguise. The regimen gives Helena an urgently distended bladder, embarrassing on the job because she is forever leaving her post to go to the bathroom. Inevitably the phone rings, and she isn't there to answer it. She has caught on recently that the answering of phones is a duty expected of her, although there are no formal titles in the office. "Everyone here is an associate," Helena was told her first day, and at once she pictured a set of business cards emblazoned with her name, comma, *Associate*, Elihue and Associates, in a smart brass dispenser poised at the front of her desk. This has never materialized. She's no mere receptionist, they assure her; however, she is *the person in charge of reception*. Who has to pee every five minutes, it seems.

Helena sprints back in time to catch the phone on its third ring. After the fourth ring, the call will automatically transfer to the back office, revealing Helena's absence from her desk to the woman she is pretty sure is her boss. Breathless, she blurts out "Hello?" forgetting the prescribed greeting.

Luckily, it's only Patty. "Busy?" she asks.

"Not bad. I can talk. Most of them are still at lunch."

"Have you eaten?" Patty polices her somewhat.

"Inquiring minds want to know," says Helena. "Well, I made the mistake of eating asparagus, and now every time I pee, it smells like asparagus." A sharp, reedy scent oddly undiluted by the massive amounts of water she has drunk.

"Asparagus and . . . ?" Patty prompts, for a confession of hollandaise sauce.

"Pinch of herb salt. Gallons of water. I swear that's it."

"Jesus, aren't you still hungry? You've got two more carbs coming your way."

"Saving them for later." Nights are the hardest, so Helena occasionally shores up, even though she knows it's a bad time to take in calories.

"Good. I haven't had anything but celery and hot tea," Patty replies. "That means Len can take us out to a restaurant like normal folks."

Not another dinner with the Tycoon, thinks Helena. Patty has to pick birdlike at her salad, then proclaim, "I couldn't possibly eat another bite!" When the Tycoon goes to the bathroom, she downs her side cup of vinegar-and-oil dressing like a shot of liquor. She hides a dinner roll in her purse. She does not always eat the dinner roll, she assures Helena. She takes it just to be subversive; she really does want to keep the weight off.

Helena tries to excuse herself from all this by saying, "Mag's supposed to call me tonight."

Patty is silent for a moment, then says, "Well then, you couldn't possibly *do* anything, not if you're going to get a *phone call.*"

Helena says nothing. It's the truth, though framed in the meanest possible way.

"There's this friend of Len's . . ." Patty begins.

"Oh, no. No way."

"Let me finish, please. This friend of Len's is real nice and not looking for anything but a night out with friends. And actually, I think he kind of has a thing for big women. His first wife was big as a barn, Len says. His last girlfriend I know wore queen-size hose, because I saw them hanging in his bathroom."

"Listen to what you're saying to me. Just a friendly evening and he likes fat girls."

"Just come and meet a man on the outside," tempts Patty. "Just come and see what that's like."

"I *know* what that's like. I do. Visiting hours are never over." Helena is joking, but a part of her has really grown accustomed to this setup. She doesn't much envision a life with Mag on the outside, though they do speak of it. She knows she has always settled for what she could get in the way of a man and that Mag is pretty much just that: what she can get. But it's working out all right. He is reasonably cute and kind; he calls when he can, wants to know what she's been doing. She enjoys the certainty of knowing at all times where he is, the dependable regularity of Sunday visits. Sometimes she wants more but reasons that, in all things, controlled portions are good for her.

"You know, Len says you have a real pretty face," Patty says.

"There's a big BUT tacked onto the end of that"—Helena laughs—"because I have a big butt." An old joke.

"Oh, we're so funny today," Patty sniffs. "The asparagus must be such an amusing vegetable."

Helena should have seen this coming; Patty has always wanted her to do everything she does. After Clint got locked up, Patty begged, *Come with me, Helena, please; I just can't stand to go alone.* And then: *Helena, don't you like that wiry little cuss Mag? Wouldn't it be odd but in a nice way not so terrible if we both had a reason to go?* Helena knows she has generally caved in to Patty's wishes, almost as much from not having strong preferences of her own as from Patty's unrelenting nature. Though, unlike Patty, she didn't marry, Helena reminds herself. Even at her heaviest, she could have gotten married. Patty was fatter than Helena when she married Clint. Their lives are simply different. Helena is dropping weight now too, but at her own pace. She's thinking she will be satisfied by size fourteen, while Patty shrinks resolutely into nothingness.

"I'll come, all right?" Helena sees she can afford to give in, that this is nothing but a meal, one she can almost enjoy because someone else will pay, and she has eaten only asparagus.

Helena's "associates"—an apt term, since none are really friends—are drifting in, sated from lunch, their grease and salt smells wafting through the office, so she says goodbye to Patty.

All afternoon, hunger sloshes around in her belly, liquid and anxious. She gulps more water: warm, cold, lemoned, plain. Her bladder stretches; it, too, must learn discipline. She won't go to the bathroom until she has answered three calls, then five, then seven, nine, twelve. Taut, waterlogged, at last she goes to the bathroom and releases a deluge of clear urine. The asparagus smell is gone. This is the cleansing power of water.

Helena thinks of her new dress: gossamer light, brightly flowered, a cut that does nothing to diminish size but does flatter shape somewhat, floating at midcalf, poofed at the sleeves. An almost dangerous swoop at the neckline, lace trim resting on the ledge of her breasts. Not a caftan, not a smock, but a real dress, purchased at the department store, not from a catalog. She'd planned to premiere this dress on her next visit with Mag, but why not wear it tonight? Pure, bloated, buoyed into evening, Helena goes home.

The restaurant is the richly paneled, brass-accented steak-and-lobster type preferred by the Tycoon and his ilk. He has brought Patty and Helena here before, or to another place just like it. Helena considers the appetizers, while the Tycoon's friend looks on approvingly. She can't even remember the last time she has ordered an appetizer. People tend to stare frankly at your plate when you're fat; Helena has sensed their curiosity, amusement, and outrage. It's as if she is behaving audaciously by eating in public at all. The diet club suggests a glass of tomato juice or half a grapefruit prior to a meal, or meditation. Fatty tidbits on tiny plates are utterly forbidden, but she will have some nonetheless. Shrimp cocktail? Stuffed mushrooms? Escargot? "That's snails, right?" she asks the Tycoon's friend. His name is Kev.

"You betcha." He squeezes her arm, then pats it with jovial affection. Several times tonight, Kev has squeezed her arm, friendly enough, though his grip seems a little hungry, like the Hansel and Gretel witch feeling for meat on the bones. He does indeed like big women. Helena thinks of Mag grasping her thigh under the picnic table, and it gives her an unexpected jolt of pleasure.

"And calamari rings. That's squid, right?"

"Um, I think."

"Want to try some? Want to split?"

"Fried, Helena." Patty cautions weakly.

Helena turns to Kev. "This is a special occasion, right?"

"You better believe it." Kev pats her hand, a double beat. Then her knee. A tentative squeeze. His eyes shine, taking all of her in. Kev is a large man, but not extremely so; fairly tall and broad-shouldered, beer gut tidily constrained by a belt. His hair is thinning but still there, neatly combed. He seems fairly regular and nice; he just has this thing for big women. Mag, she realizes, seems almost indifferent to her size; he has started teasing her only since she began her diet, when he saw that it mattered to her. What she is to Mag isn't really body, Helena concludes. It's comforts that *include* the body, but it isn't body. She doesn't know exactly what it is, but she feels a twinge of guilt for coming here.

"Surf-and-turf," the Tycoon keeps saying. "Surf-and-turf for everybody. All diets are off." He's plotting something for tonight. His bolo tie is the special one Patty says he wears only to important deals, the clasp an emerald-encrusted lizard with ruby eyes. He orders the most expensive wine and keeps craning his neck to glance furtively toward the kitchen.

"No surf-and-turf for the girls," protests Patty. "You know that's way off limits," but she's gnawing her lip. When the waitress comes, Patty lets the Tycoon order for her, nodding helplessly. Helena decides on shrimp cocktail and prime rib, medium rare.

After several glasses of wine, and several toasts by Kev, "to the lovely ladies"—*squeeze*—he acts as if could plump the pillows of Helena's breasts and roll into her like bedtime. Patty and the Tycoon wear the sneaky-smug grins of conspirators, but no matter. The food starts arriving. Pink beckoning fingers of shrimp curl around the rim of a squat goblet of red sauce. The rolls gleam with butter. The soup is rich broth beneath a crust of browned cheese. Helena feels the small, sleek bodies of shrimp in her mouth, glossy liquids, steam misting her brow. She tastes everything, even the brown speckled mustard in a pottery jar on the centerpiece, but she doesn't lose control. It is enough just to sample things; she knows she hasn't missed out. Halfway through her prime rib, she has a sensation that she can't identify at first, it seems so premature: She's full.

"Stick a fork in me," she tells the table. "I'm done." She dabs lightly at her forehead with her napkin, beaming at everyone, even the skinny waitress who lingers an extra beat with the dessert tray. That's when composure usually breaks, Helena realizes. Half a sandwich, then half a cherry pie. But she simply isn't hungry anymore.

"Just coffee, please," Helena says benignly. Then, to the others: "I don't know how that scrawny little thing lugs those big trays around. She must take a lot of vitamins."

"I like this woman," Kev tells the others, more confidently squeezing and patting Helena, who becomes keenly aware of another sensation: irritation.

The Tycoon dings his fork against his wineglass. "Hear ye, hear ye," he begins, and his tanned face shrivels into silent giggles. He has drunk enough to be easily amused with himself.

"Oh, Len," Patty admonishes, but her eyes are bright, her mouth smeared red with steak sauce.

"My friends, we are gathered here together"—the Tycoon snorts, barely constraining his laughter—"to witness a very special occasion, it being the proposal of . . that is, from—um—me to you. Damn it, I've started too soon." He signals wildly to the maître d', who scurries over to Patty with a covered platter.

"Madame, I don't believe you've seen all our desserts," the maître d' recites, and lifts the lid with an attempted flourish that fails; the metal lid slips through his fingers and knocks the platter out of his other hand. Both clatter as they hit the floor, and the lid rotates loudly on its rim for a long minute. Finally, the maître d' stops it with his foot. The plate is empty. Everyone watches him expectantly.

"Shit," he mutters, dropping to his knees. He fishes around under the table, then retrieves a small box and hands it to Patty.

"Oh my God!" she shrieks unconvincingly, lifting the lid. She jams the ring onto her finger, and the Tycoon embraces her.

"Champagne!" he demands, and the maître d', sheepish, retreats to the kitchen and quickly returns, bottle in hand. Patty displays her ring to all, a garish chunk of diamond glinting harshly in the candlelight.

"Good Lord, you'll blind somebody with that!" Helena exclaims. Patty titters proudly. The band is a little tight on her finger, Helena notices, but she has no doubt it will be floating loose on the bone by the day of the wedding.

"A toast," announces the Tycoon, "and then I am taking my lovely bride-to-be away from all this."

Helena tilts her glass heavily into Kev's, hoping to slosh some champagne into his lap. "Cheers," she murmurs, a little stricken.

Kev's lower lip quivers with emotion. He turns to Helena. "It's fantastic, isn't it? You knew, didn't you? Oh, man. Love. That's what it's all about, huh? Two people thrown together in the middle of all the madness, and it's just a beautiful, beautiful"— she watches the meaty claw descend— "thing." *Clamp.*

She pinches his leg hard enough to make him gasp, and he stops midsqueeze. Then she applies several stinging slaps to the injured leg, grinning broadly in mean parody, making her eyebrows dart up and down in exaggerated lechery. "I have a boyfriend," she whispers loudly in his ear. Kev laughs nervously and gives her arm a final, delicate pat.

"Maybe this is a bad time to bring it up," Helena continues, "but I guess I'll be needing a ride home." Without a plump limb to squeeze or pat, he is reduced to toying with his leftovers. He nods sullenly but soon musters up enough cheer to offer the Tycoon one of those manly-handshake half-hug grapples.

Patty gives Helena an excited squeeze. "We'll get real tomorrow," she promises, which probably means a couple of things: they'll talk about all this, and they'll seriously atone at the diet club. The Tycoon leads her away.

"So where's this *boyfriend?*" Kev demands bitterly of Helena as they make their way alone to the parking lot.

"Purdue County Correctional, if you must know." This effectively silences him until they're in the car and a good distance down the road.

Finally, with forced casualness: "So what's he in for?"

"Stealing cars. That's not all of it, but that's all I know." Stealing lots of cars, she explains, supposedly to be whisked across the border or to be broken down into parts and recombined into untraceable cars. But really, she knows, Mag stole cars because he had a special knack. He carried a knowledge in his fingers that allowed him to caress an unfamiliar steering column and find the vulnerable spots. "Do what you love, and the money will follow," he advised her once, unusually inspirational-book-like, when Helena was looking for a new job. Though Clint has told her that Mag was never very profitable, because he was selective about stealing cars in too personal a way. He went for the ones that challenged him most, which is why he's locked up now, or at least partly why. Helena suspects he still mourns for swiping cars, that his fingers ache and twitch at night. Mag has his own hungers to bear.

"You know, I think you could do better than that," Kev observes, some of his earlier fondness returning.

Helena considers it. Maybe she could get all Patty has gotten. It might be interesting to see. But something in her wants to reject all of it, most especially this date offered to her out of her cousin's magnanimous pity.

"You can drop me off," Helena decides as he pulls into her neighborhood, nearing the street where she lives. A fat moon is glinting off the rooftops, a row of sparkling houses all leading to hers. She'll walk, not to make up for dinner, but to feel her calves flex and her blood move, to feel as if she's moving toward something. She can see it from here.

THE WATER MAN

My granddaughter, Claire, has lately been fussing about the bad-tasting drinking water here; doubly fouled, she claims, by fertilizer leaking into the supply, which is then run through lead pipes into our rusty basin. First of all, it's the same water I've been drinking for years, good, fresh well water, so cold your teeth ache. Secondly, I am hardly able to afford this fancy system she wants to put in. Now, if she wants to put aside some of the considerable money she is saving from not having to pay rent here, well, she's got my blessing.

Of course, Claire does not want to. She says she'll make do with bottled water for the time being and hope that I come to my senses. Well. My response is this: Get started on that doctored water, and pretty soon you won't be able to stand anything else. So? she says. So, I say, when you can't get any, then where will you be? And just *why* would I not be able to get any? she shoots back, in that stubborn sulk so like her daddy's that I can hardly stand it, I love her to pieces. I whipped her daddy's mean little tail, though, when he was a boy, for being half as smart.

But I could never spank Claire; I don't think anyone could, and it's probably number one why she smarts off as much as she does now, and number two why she can't get along with anybody. That ex-husband of hers, well, I'll never excuse such behavior, and both of them were too young anyhow. But Claire can get right in your face with something, and just because we never hit her didn't mean nobody would.

"Listen," I tell her. "Middle of the night. Lean times. There you'd be, parched. And all that running water right nearby, only it doesn't taste good anymore." I tell her how I stayed in a boardinghouse when I first left home. It had a regular faucet, the first I'd seen. I worked the handle up and down like at the pump and my landlady about bust her gut laughing. I appreciate modern plumbing, but it's not good enough for Claire.

So the water man comes for a demonstration. He shows me a plastic cup full of muck he *claims* to have filtered out of our water. I'm impressed but not pulling out the checkbook just yet. He's good-looking enough, polite, but has two fingers gone at the knuckle that I'm this close to asking about. Him and Claire start talking about the ecology, though, and I scoot out of the kitchen to let them hit it off if they will. No one's going to accuse me of interfering.

I step outside to check on my snapdragons, which the heat has nearly taken, and can't help but notice his van, which looks clean and fairly new. Probably just the company van, but I like to see a well-kept vehicle. I think it says something about a man's character. My husband kept our car sparkling; you could literally eat right off the hood. I wander a little closer to maybe catch a peek at the insides and notice that the driver-side window is sealed over with a sheet of plastic. Also, there's this baby shoe hanging from the rearview mirror. I get a funny feeling and go back in to hurry things along.

Claire has fixed them each a glass of lemonade—with the doctored water, I'm guessing. She's unbuttoned the collar of her blouse and tucked her hair behind both ears, her nervous fingers a bad sign; I know she's taken with him. The water man, on the other hand, is making himself mighty comfortable in my kitchen.

"Remember, Claire, you have to drive me into town," I say, and give her what I hope is a meaningful glance.

"News to me," says Claire, twirling her bangs.

"Mrs. Mangum," says the water man, "what do you think?" He swirls that murky junk in the plastic cup at me again, and I can't help now but stare at his stubs of fingers. "Ready to get rid of those impurities? This system will do you up right." He's got a slick radio-announcer voice, and all kinds of alarms go off in my head.

"What happened to your window?" I ask, and fix him with a knowing look, like, I am on to you, mister. "One of your customers do that?"

I catch him off guard, but just for a second. He laughs, big and heavy. "Oh, that. Most unprofessional, I realize. The remains of an unpleasant altercation," he says, one of those explanations so hidden in big words as to be no explanation at all. "What if I promise to have it repaired before I take your granddaughter to dinner tonight?" He looks over at Claire, and his eyebrows arch up and flatten back out. I reckon he thinks that's becoming.

I reckon Claire does too, because she nearly strangles on her lemonade. But she recovers quick and says, "Where?"

I get out of the kitchen. Later, I notice all these jugs of water in the refrigerator. Maybe it's my imagination, but the lemonade does taste sweeter than usual.

A little homemade cherry wine is sour-sweet and quells the ache in old bones. It makes your heart floaty and singing. My one good neighbor brings me a quart jar of it near the end of every summer, and it is the only time I imbibe now, though I used to take a cocktail every now and again. My husband would say, "What'll it be, darlin'?" and I would say, "A Manhattan, if you please," even though I didn't know what went in one and he fixed us each a bourbon and Coca-Cola no matter what the request. I just liked to say Manhattan, because it was a sophisticated and faraway place. At the other end of the spectrum, a little cherry wine is right at home.

"Purely medicinal," I say, and tip my glass to Claire, who does the same. She bought us pretty goblets to drink out of, but the wine looks thick as blood in them, and the floating specks call more attention to themselves somehow. I am slightly embarrassed to be seen on the porch with goblets, besides.

"We had a Chardonnay with dinner last time," Claire says, and her eyes are faraway bright already, not the wine's doing. This will be their fifth dinner by now.

"I don't know what that is," I complain. I don't. I know it's probably wine, unless we're way off the subject, but I don't want her talking past me about this man.

"It's wine, and it's sheer liquid gold," she says, not even the littlest bit irritated. "It's perfect with chicken, which is what he had, or fish, which is what I had."

"What's good with a corned beef sandwich?" I ask, and answer my own self: "Cherry wine." I'm thinking of fixing corned beef sandwiches for dinner. Claire is humming something sweet and lazy and not even hearing me.

"Is he left-handed or right-handed?" I ask, hinting about the fingers. "I'm trying to picture him cutting his meat."

If she knows how he lost the fingers, she doesn't volunteer. "That water treatment system is his very own independent business venture," she tells me instead, and I am not unimpressed.

Still. "Does that mean we're going to have to buy one?" I ask. I don't like doing what I'm trying to do, which is needle her into defending him, but we are not the type of family that says, "Oh, how delightful. Please tell me more about this young gentleman that you are so smitten with." That is not how we get the facts.

"You know what?" she says suddenly. "I love you and I appreciate you letting me stay in your home," and she kisses my cheek, leaving me with nothing to say. Oh yes, she can use her therapy words on me, but I'm not the one she took the therapy for. It was for men of all walks.

We sip quietly a little while, and then we lapse into the kind of woman talk which, if anyone else heard, would mortify me, truly. I tell Claire about my growing up years. "It's true we were kept ignorant; I mean, I didn't know a thing. When I had my first menstruation, I thought I was dying from my privates. I dripped blood in the snow from the house to the shed, where I buried my bloomers, but the dog dug them up and drug them all over the yard. Mama gave me some clean cotton rags and safety pins and said this would be happening from now on and not to just throw away a decent pair of bloomers every time it did."

Claire falls out laughing every time I tell this. Her dumb old grandmama. Her own mama gave her a set of books before Claire even had the merest mention of titties. They had color pictures of people's privates with all the inside tubes and even a baby growing in a woman's stomach. I don't know but that seeing all of that wouldn't have just messed me up more. Claire's been wearing tampons since she was twelve, as it was summertime when she started, and she wanted, no, *needed* to go swimming. Too much too soon, I thought.

"The neighbor lady," Claire reminds me. She is shaking with held-over giggles, and I love to see her pretty white teeth when she lets loose.

I say, "There was this lady that visited with Mama—this was right around the time of the dog dragging my bloomers. She must have had a lot of female problems; it was *my vagina* this and *my vagina* that. I thought it must be some precious possession, like a fur coat or a silk hat, that called for such frequent upkeep and mention. Her people were well-off, you see, and she was forever going on about things like *credenzas* and *valances* and *foyers*. It was a whole other language. One day I was sitting in the kitchen with Mama and her, being a nice young lady, and when she brought it up again I said I would sure like to have myself a vagina. Mama only said hush—she never let on that I already had one! I don't think I knew that until your daddy was born." Claire positively hoots.

I'm putting her on a little. I think I knew well enough about what I had once I was married. I maybe didn't have the words. The point is, I know plenty now, things and names of things both, and Claire shouldn't think she's fooling me about the water man.

"You shouldn't think you're fooling me," I say.

I know that she sneaks him in late and they are intimate on my living room couch. I also know that he is not yet divorced and that the "altercation" that broke his window involved his wife and a brick. The wife's mother, who it turns out goes to my church, set me straight on the whole thing last Sunday. The baby shoe is still a mystery, as she did not mention any children. But I've learned enough to hold the reasonable belief that he is trouble.

"You're not fooling me," I say again, but that's all I say, and Claire is still laughing about her most ignorant grandmother in the whole wide world.

"Tell me about you and Granddaddy Willard," she says, settling down. "About when you were first together."

I'm glad to tell it. "When your granddaddy used to come calling," I say, "he'd wait out my other callers; he'd stay late, until my landlady practically shooed him away with a broom. 'This here is a respectable place,' she claimed, but that didn't stop the wind blowing right through the walls, nor the rats neither, nor them powdered eggs she fixed. But he kept coming and staying on, waiting me out until I finally agreed to marry him."

"He was a good-looking man," she reminds me.

"Mercy, yes. He was easy on the eyes. He was a tall man, which is where you get your height. Sea-green eyes, but you got my hazel. He kept a tan, but you got mine and your daddy's allergic white skin."

"I got his hair, though, right?" Claire says.

"Finger-in-the-electric-socket hair," I agree. "Oh yes. And his dainty little nose and ears. Yours turn red just like his. They're red right now," I tease her. "Better lay off the cherry wine."

"They're not," she says, but she touches the back of her hand to them just the same. Her wristwatch reminds her of the time, and she hops up quick to go get ready, I assume for her date.

I'm sad she's going; I feel like I am just getting started on me and Willard. Claire reminds me of me. How everything's a wonder right at the first, but I should warn her how you can just get so used to a man. Not right away, but soon enough, I was going around in housedresses. Married, I had Willard all the time, you see. Then his moods became not so charming.

Claire's daddy had the colic, and sometimes Willard would warn me, "My head is about to bust, Bedelia." And what would happen when it did, I sure wasn't going to find out. I would rock that wailing child on the back porch, or walk him between the rows of beans in the garden. The sun would go down, and I didn't dare go back in the house until that baby got quiet. And when Willard was out of work, well, there was no question, no point in even bringing it up, though I could have had my telephone operator's job back. No, he'd sooner us go hungry; he'd sooner our little boy wear his shoes given out in the toes. And do you think he'd wear one of those things or else abstain? No, and so I had another baby, Rosella, and one that didn't make it. Willard named her Pearl and had them put it on the headstone, but I named her nothing. She wasn't here long enough to be burdened with a name.

Then when Willard went off to the war, I just longed for even the smallest taste of him. My mind kept latching onto little things he'd done that were sweet: the way he said, "Bedelia, you've just got to marry me," like he would die; how he doted on his children when they didn't cry; how he always got me something pretty on my birthday. "I like you decorated up nice," he told me. And he was good to look at. Yes sir. But he didn't come back from the war, and I'll never have him again, not in this world. That was thirst. I could have gotten another husband, I know, but to carry on with little children in the house! I soon lived on a block of widows, and some did take up with other men. I didn't think bad of them, but it was not for me. Still, my waist stayed just as little as before my babies. I took my time going gray. Even now I'm told I look good for my age, but I could do without the disclaimer. Sometimes I cursed my husband for going off and getting himself killed. He had his unreasonable notions, Willard did, his heated moments and his unrelenting nature, but for a while after he was gone, they were just the things I wanted.

Cherry wine makes you sweet and mournful in remembrance. It lends you forgiveness. When the water man pulls up, honking, I give him a second-chance friendly wave that belies all my suspicion and concern, and I go inside to hurry Claire along. "Sugar, you look real pretty," I tell her. "Run on, now. He's waiting for you." Why shouldn't the ones that have someplace to go, go? That's what young is: going going gone.

Did I say that?

Things are revving up. She's gone to work and then she's home—got to lay down, got to have her a nap—and then, poof! Gone again. I notice that the water man has yet to have fixed his window glass. The plastic has come aloose and flaps in the wind as they drive off to Lord knows where, not even to get a decent meal anymore, likely. I believe they're past civilized courting over meals. She'll soon be skinny again, like when she got separated from her husband and showed up at my door. Where else was she going to go but here, with her mama re-married and moved out of the state and her daddy remarried—not once; three times. I guess I know where she learned to get a divorce. Something not right, you just cash it in, never mind about the vows you made in front of God and everybody else. Ought to have a supermarket for those kind of weddings, or a drive-by like the McDonald's. Of course, people have their reasons. Somebody mean all the time to you is a good reason.

It's getting real late, and I'm kind of upset, but Claire doesn't know I wait up for her, so what can I say? Claire tells people she stays on here to look after me, but I still drive and I still eat solid food and they're my criteria for living independent. I've got the *perspective* she doesn't, but I reckon we both need a little and are needed. I still drive all right, but parking's getting trickier. Still, it's been *me* sorting out *her* life mostly, me being watchful and listening, me looking through the classifieds for something better—she says she likes the dime store fine, but she's never even tried for anything else since she's been here. A year is enough clerking and shelving for anybody with half a mind.

I believe they drink to excess when they are out so late, because they come back on the tail end of a fight, whisper-shouting in the dark. There's a struggle, and I listen hard for the sounds to turn loving, so I know she's not being hurt. I don't yet believe she is, but it's a dangerous dance that goes on down there in my living room.

And in the daylight, all I hear is her overwhelming nostalgia and appreciation for this place. "This is the town of my youth," she has been declaring lately. "I was never anything but happy here. I may not ever leave again." While she's welcome to stay here as long as she likes, this convenient new outlook is troubling. Town of her youth! Anything but happy is more like it. Either her mama or her daddy, one was dropping her off here for undetermined lengths. When she finally got past crying for them, a deep and abiding boredom would settle over her. She didn't want to go to Sunday school, didn't want to help in the garden or the kitchen, didn't want to go to the grocery store or the park or the movie. Television on night and day, slack-jawed—a more sullen, moping child I never have seen, but bless her heart, she couldn't help it. Her parents took their long and messy time parting. Maybe coming here was a kind of break for her, but at the time, I know, she didn't like it, or me much. It worries me when people redo their memories.

I thought my memories would fade out with time, but they loom. A little bigger, even, than some of the more recent things. I'm a little startled sometimes when I walk into my living room and the furniture is all wrong. It was bought ten years ago, but I am still expecting the matching velveteen couch and chair Willard got us on credit when we were first married, not all this plaid, not this shag rug. Same with the car: I am looking for green-gold all-American big and swollen, shiny with chrome and a fresh wax, but instead there is a small tan box parked in my driveway, dull as dirt. And now Claire's teeny yellow truck. I see it and start, thinking: Who's here? Oh yes; that's my grand-baby, who's got no business even being old enough to drive a car. I will sometimes even wonder where my children are. It seems my arms still hold the ache of a baby squirming in them. Children should be messing at the table or out rowdy in the yard, Willard hollering for them to cut that racket, he means pronto!

And this bed. The headboard is the same; my head bumped this deep polished maple on my wedding night; but mine is the only body to wear a hollow in the orthopedic mat-tress. I go to sleep in the dead center of it, but in the night some-times I scoot over and find myself patting for Willard, needing to rest my hand on the flat of his belly before I pick up the thread of my dream again. He isn't there, of course, but for a minute it's because he's still out with his buddies, then it's because he's gone to the war, and finally it's because he's a long time dead, and I settle back into the snug center spot I have made for myself and rest easy.

I'd likely do the same tonight, but for Claire. I won't have peace until her absence is rectified. She can pull me right back into the now.

"Mama Beddy," Claire calls. "Your breakfast is getting cold." Those days when I am up with the sun are over. I need my rest.

But a body also needs some bacon crisp-frying in a pan mornings, and when Claire gets up and fixes, it's oatmeal and fruit, a little coffee if I'm lucky. She's got that classical music station going, and I make like I'm an opera singer along with it, only my voice hasn't come full in yet, so it's just a sound like ungreased hinges. "Oh please," she says.

"I've got to have me an egg," I tell her, and make for the refrigerator.

"You sit," she says. "I'm boiling you an egg if you've got to have one." Like she's doing me a favor. I'd just as soon make my own breakfast if I don't have any say.

"You're up early, considering," I observe, mildly enough, but she goes almost cross-eyed at that.

"Considering?"

"Considering your date."

"Mama Beddy, you know I've got to work this morning. You know I've got to eat a good breakfast so my hypoglycemia doesn't act up."

That doesn't explain why we're eating this and not a good breakfast, though of course I don't say that. But something in my face must say it when she sets that oatmeal in front of me, because she flings down her spoon right pouty after a minute and huffs, "Well, just what is it you'd rather have? Brains and eggs, no doubt. Big slab of ham fried in lard."

"Grits and redeye gravy," I say in fond remembrance. "Bacon. Two eggs sunny side to dip my biscuit in. We weren't much for brains and eggs. Just after slaughter."

Her face screws up tight at that.

I tell her, "You need to get more sleep. You've got a sour disposition in the morning."

"I don't need to remind you I am a grown woman," she says tightly.

"I know you're grown! Already been married once."

Claire is quiet, but the air is thick between us. I suppose I'm a little sour myself, so I decide to pull a switch and try her tactic of killing with kindness.

"I appreciate your fixing breakfast," I say. "Maybe it's not what I'd of chosen, but I know you look after my health better than I do." I slurp up a big spoonful of bland soggy oatmeal without sugar or milk. "I believe I will have that boiled egg," I add; I am literally mealymouthed.

Claire is spitting fire, but she gets up to do it, letting the pot bang into everything it can on its way from the cabinet to the sink to the stove.

I say, "I'll return the favor and cook you a good dinner tonight."

Claire answers with her back to me. "There's no need to trouble. I already have dinner plans."

"Aren't you sick and tired yet of restaurant meals?" I say. "Ask your friend to have dinner with us."

"Why should I?" she blazes, whirling around. "It's clear you think he's some kind of criminal."

"Claire, I think no such a thing," I say with great dignity. I am too affronted to finish this lukewarm mush without maple syrup, so I snatch the bottle from the pantry and squeeze a big dollop into my bowl. "I haven't had the chance to develop any opinion whatsoever about this young man." Not entirely true; I know he can sure kick up driveway gravel in his comings and goings, which shows no respect for me. I know he hasn't any respect for my granddaughter, or he'd at least spring for a motel room. Or what's wrong with his house, I'd like to know? Or even that van? Although I suppose it's filled with fragile unsold water purifier systems. So yes, I have begun to form my own opinions, but it has already occurred to me that a cordial man in a pressed shirt and maybe tie, holding my granddaughter's hand under the table and asking for second helpings, could go a long way toward changing them.

"You ask him," I insist. "I'll behave myself."

She won't ask him, but all the same I have made a pound cake and bought a good ham while she was at the bookstore today. I pinned it with pineapple slices and cloves and am just going to heat it through again, when she comes home and wrinkles up her nose.

"Is that what I think it is?" she says, glowering in my kitchen doorway.

"You've got eyes," I say. "What do they tell you?"

"They tell me I'm looking at a week of leftovers."

"That's what you think." I let the oven door slam for effect.

At sunset, I march right out to the van as he's pulling up and ask him my own self. I jerk aside that flap of plastic and say, "I know you want some good ham." The pure astonishment on his face is a pleasure. I give him the smile I usually reserve for the minister. "Come on in to dinner," I coax. What else can he do but follow me in, helpless?

Claire is on the porch, glaring at us.

"Don't you shoot them daggers at me," I tell her, and he laughs. I want to think it is because we are of a like nature, and so I link my arm in his as if I need assistance up the steps. His shirt's untucked and he's wearing dungarees, but he looks clean, and I can't ask for better, since I did ambush him. He didn't know he was going to be eating dinner with Claire's grand-mama.

"How's the water purifying business?" I ask, cutting thick slabs of the ham. I'd ask him to carve, but it might embarrass him if he didn't know how to do it right. I hate to have somebody hackling up my good ham, besides.

"You don't want to know," he says, a little sullen.

"There's a lot of people interested," Claire pipes up.

"Interested don't pay the *rent*, darlin'," he says, and I feel something clenched behind his words.

He doesn't have the hearty appetite I was so hoping for, just eats the one slice of ham and about a spoonful of potato salad. He doesn't care for peas, Claire explains. Claire eats only yogurt: she's going to sit through this dinner, but if she eats what I've fixed, she loses face. He leaves the slice of cooked pineapple—my favorite part—on his plate, and for a minute I see it like he does: brownish, wrinkled, and forlorn. He is not so comfortable in my kitchen this time, and I figure it's because, number one, I am in it, and number two, he's not trying to sell me anything. I wish he was trying to sell me something, like sell me on the idea that he is a proper fellow just crazy about Claire.

"So where are you all off to tonight?" I say, just to make conversation. He looks to Claire, and she says, "Oh, we sort of figure it out as we go. Maybe a party?" His eyebrows shoot up. "You know," she reminds him. "My boss's house. You said we'd maybe go."

"A party sounds real nice," I say. I hate the idea of them just winging it. That's no kind of date. "I know," I say. "You can bring that cake."

"If we go," says Claire, looking at him. He doesn't say anything.

"I'll just wrap up a few slices," I say, and hop up to do it.

"Claire, I'm not going to no party," I hear him say to her, low, almost growly.

"You know, maybe I am tired of sitting by myself while you get drunk and play pool with your friends." She's talking low too, but she says it kind of singsongy and sweet, like we could mistake her words for something else.

"I'll just wrap it up for you two to eat it later if you don't go," I tell them, but he is already standing.

"Mrs. Mangum, I thank you for dinner," he says in his sales-man's voice, and out the door he goes.

We hear his revving, we hear his gravel spray. Claire looks at me hard.

"Don't you say a word," she says. "Not a goddamn word," and she is out the door after him before I can even think of any-thing to say.

I think of something. "Don't be too late. You've got to work in the morning," my voice so small in this empty kitchen.

I don't want this for her, to think that this is just part and parcel of being somebody's girl. Not when I think of the bit-terness I swallowed for the privilege of being a wife. Now, I loved my husband, and I'll allow he was a good provider, but in the years since his passing I have taken on a righteousness that would no longer tolerate his voice raised to me in anger. I would no longer abide his back turned to me. Not even for the pleasure of his voice, not even for the pleasure of his body. If I could somehow press that into her, or remind her of what she's already got. I know it took something strong to get her away from the first one. She didn't just reel here all the way from Pensacola on the force of his slap. She pushed her own self up and out.

I eat off all the pineapple before wrapping up that good ham. I'm going to fry it for breakfast, sandwich it for lunch, and casserole it for dinner, and Claire can eat it or not. I'm going to use it right up.

WORDS FOR WHAT SHE WANTED

~~~

Talking was such a poor substitute for sex, Edwina was starting to think, though she did either with what appeared to be grace and aplomb, the way she sang at her sister Allison's wedding and waltzed with her arthritic father. "Truly radiant," her father said of both his daughters that day. "Call it *fucking*," said her Valium-giddy sister, Allison, in the dressing room beforehand. "That's what it is." Edwina cringed at the rude smack of the word, a sound made at even the thought of it, and inwardly revised. She preferred *abandon* or *reverie*, as much for their lurid paperback quality as their toppling syllabics. She was imperious about language but humble in other respects. "It doesn't take much to get me lost," she said when they were heading from the church to the reception hall, and handed her map over to the best man. She was perhaps overly solicitous of the maid of honor, who was embarrassed at being chosen over the bride's own sister. But that was how Edwina was.

And she would keep talking, earnestly and long. To the man at the meat counter, his hands pink with juice. To the gaunt neighbor she met daily at the mailboxes, for so long now it was too late to ask his name. To her ex-boyfriend's mother, who still hadn't given up though Edwina had. Completely? She couldn't be certain but figured every man that followed would help clear her head of him. If only some men would follow! Billy, the son, the ex-boyfriend, had been a soft, vague pudge of a man but made a spectacular woman. Edwina went to see him at the shows sometimes, and he would fling his arms about her in greeting. No hard feelings. She would sneeze into his feather boa, worn both in mockery of and homage to the venerable drag queens of yore, and they would also talk, well into the night.

But sex, intercourse in particular, had a brute deliberateness that nothing could rival, and Edwina was beginning to annoy herself with zealous conversation. Eating helped, but not eating did more—she wanted to emaciate herself with desire. The hollow burn in her stomach was promise of that. House-sitting, she indulged her sister's cat in expensive tinned morsels of veal and pâté, the sort of treats she would deny herself. Allison and her new husband were honeymooning in Jakarta, a place chosen on the strength of a National Geographic Special. They almost didn't go because of all the shots, and Allison had her passport photo redone twice because she thought she looked squinty-eyed. Squeamish and vain. It pleased Edwina to pamper and fatten her sister's cat. Rexroth had taken to sprawling extravagantly at her feet, and she knew he would grow morose when Allison came back and tried to feed him those sordid brown pellets again. Such little vindictive acts soothed Edwina.

She was spending a lot of time at Allison's house, having volunteered for an end-of-season layoff at the order-processing center of Bass-Ackwards, the Midwest's most formidable supplier of hunting and fishing equipment. It seemed that the phone-in orders for hip waders, tackle boxes, and ensembles of the lighter summer camouflage would flood in from spring until around the end of June, then drop off suddenly. Edwina imagined the streams and woods choked with mobs of outdoorsmen on mass vacation. All the talking going on there had been starting to appall Edwina as well—all the dressing up of what should have been simple transactions, mere exchanging of numbers. She'd had to greet her callers with "Good Fishing!" and proceed from there, reaffirming their choices, buttering them up for the soft sell at the end: "Could I interest you in our Bucket o' Tender Tubes, regularly priced at twelve ninety-five; today only six dollars?" The small gasp of betrayal that came from the caller would make Edwina wince. Since it was her intention to return to school in the fall, she decided she deserved a little leisure time herself and was living on her savings until the student loan came through. This left little money for entertainment, so she worked on her tan and watched a lot of cable television. Allison's house was well equipped for both.

There was another reason to hang around Allison's house, though Edwina would deny it if asked. In one of her many ambivalent gestures, she had given Allison's phone number instead of her own to a college student she had met briefly at one of the many parties before the wedding. He did not know her sister, or her sister's impending husband, but had insinuated himself into the party on the basis of some sporadic friendship with an usher. He ate the crab legs brazenly, unashamed. He was a senior, majoring in Real Estate. Edwina's lip had curled at the sound of that, but he was dogged about refilling her drink and had an unexpectedly sexy sway to his torso when they danced. Edwina felt indulgent—but only to a point; perhaps she, too, had eaten too freely. Belly full, sated, she accepted a ride home from the student, dictated Allison's telephone number to him, and allowed one slobbery kiss to be asserted on her neck before getting out of the car.

Edwina had then felt the stirrings of a perverse dislike that may have had something to do with smell. He didn't have a bad odor, but it was distinctive and odd, more chemical than earthy. Wrong. Still, not a good enough reason to cut him off completely, not feeling the way she did. It could have been just an odd combination, she reasoned: hair gel reacting with the wrong aftershave or talc, plus the alcohol he drank exuding from his pores. Since she knew she'd been just hanging around waiting for the call, once it came she felt unable to refuse. All that loaded talk with the butcher. Lonely wasn't it, but "skin hungry," Allison's expression, came awfully close. Why look a gift horse? and so forth.

So Edwina was there for the call, and she agreed to meet him, but she wasn't sure yet if he was what she wanted. She needed an out, in case he wasn't. In preparation for their date, she spruced up one of her sordid-past stories, still dripping with pathos and full of woe. One of her desperate teenage runaway tales. She was both as animated and as removed in the telling of these as if she were recounting a movie she'd viewed long ago. Interesting enough to tell, and tell well if you were the dramatic type (and Edwina was), but after all, only a movie. The trick was to make herself appear so weird, so tragic and inaccessible, that the hapless college student would withdraw of his own accord. It was a weapon she'd keep sheathed unless called upon to defend herself.

The student's name was Kyle, and he spoke with some bitterness of his future in real estate, to Edwina's great relief.

"Not *my* choice," he lamented. "Not my choice at all." They sat at a wrought-iron table in Predilections, a shabby Victorian made over into a coffee shop. It was a pompous and expensive place, reeking of lavender sachets and vanilla-mocha-almond espresso. A cup of the house grind cost two dollars, and no free refills. Edwina twirled a tendril of bangs in her finger and waited for Kyle to say something ironic and disapproving about the place. She noted how the tilt of his eyebrows suggested a perpetual sarcasm. There were other promising features: the dark hair longish and spread across his forehead, an eyetooth that kept snagging his chapped lower lip when he spoke. She imagined herself as one more bitter bead on his string, another of many dissatisfactions. This she liked immensely.

"Nice place," Kyle said.

"You don't think it's—well, sort of full of itself?" Edwina prompted. She would give him every chance.

Kyle hesitated, unsure. "Well, it's nice for what it is, but I guess it's not my kind of hangout, really."

"I understand completely," Edwina said amiably. "Why don't we go somewhere else? To your kind of hangout, I mean."

In his car, Edwina had a brief excited flash: what if he brought her directly to his house? But it was hardly even dark out yet. He drove the few short blocks downtown and parked in front of The Antler.

"It's a little full of itself too, now that they're remodeling," Kyle half apologized. "But they've got a good pool table." He grasped her elbow lightly and ushered her through the door. Edwina liked the mild force he used on her and headed straight for the bathroom, to recover and consider new strategies. She blotted her face with a square of toilet paper and despaired at the blackheads peppering her chin. She raked a pick through her bob to fluff it out; she remembered him saying at the party how he liked her hair. She gathered her hose at each ankle and pulled, inching up gradually to smooth out her legs. She loved the squeeze of support hose, how they contained her belly and thighs, sleeked her legs, and helped fold and wedge her toes into the pointed tips of her shoes. Billy the ex loved support hose too and wore Edwina's same brand, size, and tint. Taupe, she recalled with a pang of tenderness, and emerged from the bathroom with no clear plan in mind.

Kyle had procured them a booth and a pitcher of beer, and he motioned her over. His casual wave was becoming painfully attractive.

"Tell me," she said, sliding into the booth, "whose idea was it, if not yours? Real estate."

"It's lame," Kyle said, palms out in supplication. "Dad's a realtor. Dad's paying for school. Hence, real estate."

"But what would you rather be doing?" Edwina asked.

"That's just it," he said, in that ironic tone she'd been hoping he'd assume. "Not a thing. Not a goddamn thing. So the question isn't why real estate. It's why not."

"Well, surely—" Edwina began.

"Nope, nope nope nope nope," Kyle broke in. "There's nothing. I have no job-related interests. I do have interests, hobbies and the like. Pastimes, even. But I'm afraid it's going to be real estate." He sighed deeply, but in a way that signaled the matter was closed. "How about a shot of something?" he asked. "I could stand to take the edge off." He was already up and heading for the bar, a huge, ornately carved antique with a beveled glass mirror that stretched along the length of the opposite wall. It was ridiculously out of place beneath the ceiling of Styrofoam tiles, a cheap classroom-style ceiling.

"The owner had it shipped from Australia," Kyle said, returning with two chunky shot glasses full of amber liquid. "The bar."

"I thought it had to be a transplant," Edwina said, laughing. "One of these things is not like the others," she half sang.

Kyle was quick to defend. "Well, he spent all his money getting it here, so he can't do anything else just yet," he said.

"No, no; it's marvelous," Edwina placated. "A piece like that is the center. Everything he does will have to work with it, and that won't be easy. It's very . . ." She searched for the word. "Ballsy," she concluded.

"Yes; it could ruin him," Kyle said, excited that she seemed to understand. He slid her glass over, and their fingers glanced off each other. Edwina tilted her shot back slowly so he could get a long look at her throat, which she thought of as winsome and swanlike.

"He'll need wood floors," she continued, encouraged. "And stone masonry. And frescoes." The liquor flamed in her chest. She placed two cooling fingertips at the opening of her blouse.

Kyle gaped at her, then laughed. "Let me guess. Art history. No? Um—interior design."

"Yes," Edwina lied. "But not my choice. My whole family has poor taste in furniture, and they've pinned their hopes on me."

"Not really," Kyle said sadly, filling their beer mugs.

"Just the tacky-family part," she admitted. "I'm only a sometimes student. Classes here and there, but no major. This fall, for example. Comparative Mythology. Judo for Advanced Beginners. Literature of the Left."

"Ahh," he sighed, with deep envy and approval.

They drank the pitcher, and another, and played pool. She mocked her sister's wedding ceremony for him, sang her piece in a shrill falsetto, and they aped a waltz across the concrete floor.

"Get this," Edwina told him breathlessly. "Aqua and peach. Those were the colors." Damn tacky wedding. Edwina vowed to melt her petro-taffeta dress over a slow flame and enjoy every minute.

"Huh?" said Kyle, dipping her. Their waltz was turning into a tango. He smelled just like her, Edwina was thinking, of clean, beery sweat.

"The ushers wore aqua cummerbunds," she explained, "with peach carnations as boutonnieres."

"Cummerbunds? Boutonnieres?" echoed Kyle, confused. He gripped her hips and steered her onto a barstool. He ordered another pitcher. Their knees pressed together as they drank.

If Kyle got to know her better, he would wonder about Edwina and her sister, why the meanness. Allison would be such an easy target now that she was married, Edwina could already tell. What if for, say, two, three dates in a row, Edwina were to slam her sister for Kyle's entertainment? There would be something pathological about that, surely.

"I have to pee for like the twenty millionth time," Edwina laughed, and careened toward the bathroom. The close press of her support hose made her feel swollen and puffy. As she peeled them away, heat roiled off her skin. Fairly certain they would spend the night together, she did a quick mental inventory of the state of her apartment. Was anything there that would embarrass her or spoil the mood? Errant maxipads? Grouty bathroom tiles? But she could think of nothing appalling. Should it be her apartment or his? No, not his; she wanted to retain some measure of control over the proceedings. Bladder empty, confident, Edwina strode back out to Kyle and began tentatively to stroke his earlobe.

"I'm not sure I should drive," he confessed.

"We'll walk," Edwina assured him. "It will clear our heads."

They walked, arms encircling each other's waists. "Actually, I'm all turned around," she admitted after a couple of blocks. "Do you remember where I live?" It was a good time to reveal some vulnerability of her own, she thought.

"I remember," he said. "We're going the right way." They were silent. The cooled evening air had the bracing effect of water flung in Edwina's face, and she was no longer as sure of what would happen.

"You'll need to come in and visit awhile," Edwina said at the entrance to her building. She turned to face him and hooked her pinkies through his belt loops, risked a direct stare, as solid and unblinking as she dared.

There was an uncertain beat before Kyle mashed his lips onto hers, tongue scoring the roof of her mouth. He backed her into the building, and she rode his kiss up the stairs to her apart-ment. She did the obligatory fumbling at the lock while he lapped at the back of her neck and ears until, finally, she man-aged to get the door open. They lunged in.

The warm air inside, thick and dark, helped bring back that dreamy, boozy feeling. She guided Kyle to the couch and straddled him, skirt bunching up around her waist. He stroked her legs, her thighs. Snagging the nylon with his fingernail, he worked a hole into the crotch of her panty hose, then eased his thumb into the opening and began gently to rub, around and around. She slid her hands along his waist and began to unbutton his jeans. He stopped stroking her, grasped her hands, and brought them behind her back. He clasped her wrists together in his fist and resumed the circular motion between her thighs. She ground her hips against him, tried to find him, but he kept his hand between them, blocking contact. She gnawed at the ridges of his ears, ran her tongue along his throat. She jabbed and suckled his lips between her teeth. She tried to free her hands, to touch him, but the grip on her wrists tightened. The thumb circles quickened, spiraled inward, and she met the rhythm, turning liquid hot and cold.

Then he stopped. "Tell me what you want," he murmured in her ear. She tilted her hips against him in reply, but he wouldn't move. "No. Talk to me." She shook her wrists free.

"You know," she whispered. She raked her fingers through his hair imploringly.

"I want to hear you say it."

Only penetration, blunt and immediate, could get near the core of the thing she wanted. But she couldn't ask for that. There were other words that came close, there were ways to hint at what she wanted: *Touch this empty center; change how dead I can feel.* But she knew that as soon as she said it, the feelings would shift and elude her so she wouldn't want it anymore. Aloud would only underline what she couldn't have. She tried to kiss him instead, but he clamped his teeth shut.

"No, no," he teased. "Not until you fess up."

"Oh, I have a confession," Edwina said finally. "But I don't think you want to hear it."

Kyle gripped her buttocks eagerly. "Oh, yes I do."

"When I was sixteen," she said into his ear, low and throaty, "I was a little drugged-out slut; I didn't know what the hell was going on. There were these three guys I slept with. They were all friends. They would get me high and I would have sex with them. Separately, now; never all at once; but I didn't care which one."

Kyle's fingers crept back to the opening in her hose. Edwina continued. "Sometimes they used condoms and sometimes not. It depended on how high I was. They called me Eddie, like I was just one of the guys."

"Eddie," he murmured, and nudged a finger inside her.

"You don't want to hear the rest," she warned.

"Please, Eddie," he moaned, stabbing her with his finger.

"All right," she obliged, and rocked her hips gently. "One of these guys had his own place; he was what you'd call an emancipated minor. I stayed there sometimes, when me and my dad fought. One night he was all over my case and I said I am out of here. I went to that guy's house, the one with his own place, and the other two were there. He said I could stay as long as I wanted, I could live there, but I had to suck them all off."

Normally, Edwina would muffle a sob at this point in the telling, but she dug the heel of her hand into Kyle's crotch and felt how rigid and intent his cock was against the fabric of his jeans. Heat blossomed at the base of her spine and shuddered its way down to his finger sliding effortlessly in and out.

"This is not a sexy story," she chided, and came.

Kyle dozed off sitting up, and his head lolled over to one side. Edwina imagined he would have a terrible crick in his neck. She couldn't sleep. She felt she had to take off her panty hose; they were split open from hip to knee. She pulled them off and walked around the apartment, plucking stray items from the carpet: socks, coins, pens. Finally, she went into her bedroom and put on a fresh pair—she knew she wasn't going to sleep. Too restless, too much welling up inside. She needed a friend right now more than this near stranger, though he had helped quell something; she wasn't sure what. It would have to be sorted out later, scenes carefully replayed: what she had said and done, whether there would be consequences.

It was too soon to tell, really, but Edwina suspected that as usual she had said too much and not enough. Behind her desperate teenage runaway story, the thing that had really hurt her seemed silly compared to what she told Kyle. But it was why she'd even fought with her father and left home. Edwina had come home late on a school night, reeking of beer and pot. She had known it was a gamble: Either her father would be up waiting and pissed off, or he might have gone to bed hours earlier. This time he'd been asleep, and she breathed a sigh of relief.

But Allison was waiting up for her. *It's your turn to do the dishes, and you better do them,* she told Edwina. She held the power of disclosure. *Go to hell,* Edwina said, and Allison gleefully woke their father, who came roaring out of bed and down the hall. But at least Edwina had not done the dishes; she was too proud to do the dishes, even if she was not too proud to kneel in front of three boys, who only laughed nervously and said, *Forget it, we just wanted to see if you would,* and let her sleep on the floor.

Edwina poked Kyle gently awake. She offered him a glass of soda. He took it, wincing.

"What time is it?" he asked.

"Drink up," she urged. "I've got to take you back to your car. Or home." She kissed him on the cheek to make it seem less unfriendly. He meandered down to her car with her, in zombie acquiescence.

"Is back to your car okay?" Edwina asked cheerfully, popping the clutch. "I mean, I know where that is, and I don't know where you live, and I'm not sure you could tell me just now; am I right? But then," she reasoned, "maybe you shouldn't be driving yourself if you can't even tell me where you live, so just tell me where you live."

Kyle knuckled his eyes and yawned directions.

"Great," Edwina chirped brightly. "I'm real familiar with that street. I won't have any problem getting there or back. And tomorrow I'd be glad to take you to your car. I mean, if you don't feel like just walking over there; I mean, it's not very far. But you call me if you want a ride, and you got it, okay? I mean, if nobody else can take you. That would be fine." Her ramblings seemed to lull Kyle back to sleep, and Edwina was glad, because she really did not want to talk. At all.

Gallantly, Edwina waited for Kyle to enter his building, a sprawling apartment complex nearly identical to her own, before she drove away. He gave her a sleepy wave as he shuffled in. Edwina savored her present indifference. In a week, she would be nibbling on her memory of this night, hungry again.

But now it was other memories she wanted to sift through and be comforted by. She thought of Billy when he was her lover, thought of touching the soft curves of his face and body, feeling more like she was making love to a woman, to herself. Perhaps that was what she missed most. And now that he was so much more himself, larger than life, she could almost reach that again just being near him. Edwina felt herself honored to be allowed into both these halves of Billy's life.

She drove to the club. It was surely near closing, but the timing seemed about right for Billy or one of his costars to hear her knock at the back entrance, near the dressing area, where they were unmasking in slow stages. He'd be tired but pleased to see her, and they could just sit quietly over drinks while he applied cold cream in a circular motion and Edwina basked in their shared experiences. She felt Billy would perceive her need to just visit and not insist on too much talk. Then she could go home, sleep, and, tomorrow, assess.

As Edwina had hoped, the show was over. She tapped at the back door, was recognized and invited in. Tonight's theme had been a wedding, and most of the performers milled around in the dressing room drinking champagne, still wearing tuxe-dos, or frilly off-the-shoulder dresses and pastel wigs piled lu-dicrously high. But Billy was breathtaking, a pink-cheeked bride in a glittering white gown. He had attached his eyelashes one at a subtle time instead of pasting on the usual garish strip, and he batted them gravely beneath the shimmering veil. Foam rubber cleavage peeped innocently from his bodice. His waist was cinched to a narrow circumference, and his hips bloomed out wide in contrast. The full skirt swished dramatically when he moved. Tears came to Edwina's eyes, just as they had when she first beheld her sister in her wedding gown—before Allison started acting like a bitch, uglying the entire memory. "You're jealous," she'd accused Edwina before the wedding. "You'll never have what I have. And that's just sad, 'cause all I'm gonna have is *sex every night!*" Laughing, Allison had nearly hyperventilated, and even though Edwina knew it was the Valium talking, she hadn't forgiven her yet.

Billy's gaze came to rest on Edwina. A loving smile spread across his lightly glossed lips, and he extended both arms to her.

"And there's my maid of honor," he said.

Edwina was deeply moved. He could, she knew, intuit the rest.

"You are my one true sister," she told him.

Billy held her hands intently. "Girl," he said, "I love you and all that, but I am not your sister. I am a man."

Edwina felt the truth in what he said, but Billy was so lovely and kind. And soft; he would shape to the force of her need.

"Just for a little while," she whispered. "Just this one night." She squeezed his fingers hard, extracting nothing.

My Mama
and Me
Lose Track

I still don't know entirely what is hers and what is mine. I cut my teeth on the soft vinyl corners of her wedding album, pictures in it I can't remember ever not knowing of my pretty pretty mama in her wedding dress, ephemeral as gossamer, her waist no thicker than my ankle. Her going-away suit is complete with pert pillbox hat and matching clutch bag. She is prim and stylish and every inch a virgin. My grandmother wasn't pleased about the marriage, but there is no indication here: everyone is beaming, all the women are dressed like Jackie Kennedy. At one point, the bride and groom are smooching, playing it up big for the camera, and my grandmother is right there in the background, laughing. It's a done deal. My youngest aunt, knowing only that her big sister would be gone, sobbed through the reception and screamed, "Dell! Don't go! Please, Dell!" The rice stung them, leaving.

My parents had been high school sweethearts. I read and reread my mother's yearbook farewell to my father, signed *Love Always*, and delighted over their romance. Jim, poised in his football jersey, is slim and boyish, wholly unlike the burly, bearded father I knew, but Dell looks exactly the perfect same as my mama. I first imagined them torn apart by the cruel forces of fate, but really she was going no farther than nursing school, not half an hour from home. There is a firm finality to her letter as she wishes my father a pleasant future, good luck. She chooses to say goodbye. My sister and I exist only in abstract terms, sexless dolls wearing beatific, bow-mouthed smiles. The husband, too, is nameless. At this point, my very existence is at stake. Could some other combination have produced me? The thrill I felt reading that letter came to have less to do with curiosity about them than with the risk it implied. How easily I might never have been!

But fate interceded on my behalf, and they reconnected while she was in nursing school, enjoying the generous midnight curfews and learning to smoke cigarettes. A courtship. My mother married him, graduated, but by the first Christmas was back at my grandmother's house, alone. Already, he drank. But too late. Once you were married, you had to play the cards you were dealt. That's what her mother told her, only more kindly and with the church behind her.

She went back. My sister was born, then me. They bought a bigger house and decorated: shag rug, wood veneers, a ginger jar spewing eucalyptus sprigs, an itchy couch, a living room suite for guests and Sundays. Curtains were fitted, floors buffed, the patio sprouted a deck, the backyard grew a playhouse of the same rough-hewn, green-stained slabs as the big house. My room had a Jenny Lind bed, a bookshelf made from concrete blocks and pine planks, and a window blind red-checkered like a bistro tablecloth. Grill out on Saturday night, French toast and church on Sunday, the television always on, its massive wooden console perpetually glaring. Cold, dewy cans of beer, hundreds of them, it seemed, stored in the house's crawl space.

For a short time, my mother worked the night shift and seemed to appear only in my dreams, a beautiful ghost that embraced me and vanished. My father dressed us backward and wrong side out—all those snaps and little duck motifs unnerved him. My mother knew snaps and hooks and zippers up the back, buttons down the front. She kept a drawer filled with abandoned girdles that hooked or laced, with little clips for attaching nylons, also abandoned, in favor of panty hose—the rubbery support kind for nurses. I wore two pairs of those thick hose on cold days. They squeezed up the length of my body to my armpits. She kept a shiny black bun of hair, which she would weave imperceptibly into her own hair, perching her nurse's hat delicately atop it. Unfurled and matted, it became my Gypsy or witch wig on Halloween. She smelled of perfume and tobacco and of sweet, mediciny lotions and unguents—expensive makeup I was always dribbling into my hands and smearing on: blue creme for eyelids, pinkish red for lips, medium beige all over, rouge applied in a circular motion. I scraped my arms and legs with her pink disposable razors, I waddled around with her maxipads wedged in my underwear—their function still a mystery to me, I knew the ritual of wearing them would invoke some response in my body, the way shaving had caused the soft down to grow back bristled.

Our dog, Sam, had litter upon litter of puppies, and I witnessed the mess of birth. With gentle teeth, she peeled away the gleaming gelatinous sac to reach the puppy inside. She bit through the cord and licked away the blood. How was I made, Mama? Can't be this way, not how dogs are. Freckles jumped the fence, I called him Sam's husband. But how was I made? *The father plants a seed in the mother.* (If you swallowed a watermelon or grape seed, a vine would grow in your stomach, so I knew this to be plausible.) Mama said she carried me in her stomach until I grew big enough to come out. Where did I come out? The *vagina*—the awesome power of the word enough to sustain me then. She told me I was a good baby, fat and pleasant. My sister Karen thought I was too small to play with, so she commandeered my bassinet and shut me in the refrigerator. I ate everything, and Karen ate only applesauce. My first sentence was *Me me whole lot.* I ate vitamins, children's aspirin, and drank 409, was made to vomit with syrup of ipecac. My mother kept a swatch of my hair in an envelope, superfine soft baby hair. A box in my dad's dresser drawer held the baby teeth I worked, loosened, and jerked out of my mouth. Tiny shoes bronzed on a shelf. Splotchy handprints framed. Already I had a history, relics, an archaeology.

My mother sang: "I love you/A bushel and a peck/and a hug around the neck." She played "The Spinning Song" on the piano, and Karen and I would whirl around to it until we fell. No one could do as many things or sing better or be prettier or love me more than my mother. My father lumbered right through us, lifting and nailing and sawing things. He rasped my cheek with his beard, he shouted and doled out the spankings. Those stacks of Willie Nelson albums dropping down on the turntable, one by one. I resented the distraction he caused. He wrecked our closed and perfect circle. Karen too. They were my rivals.

But a swimming pool, we got a swimming pool! My father rented a bulldozer and gouged out the backyard, then at midnight he and his poker buddies patted sand into the walls of the hole. They lined it with blue vinyl, filled it with water, and soon I was gripping the sides all the way around, circumnavigating. Later, our collie pup fell in, and I was transfixed, frozen, thinking I should run or call for help before reaching in. But I did nothing, though it was as easy as reaching in to get her, which my sister did instantly, instinctively. I was lost inside myself already, couldn't react right. I didn't know how; I was stillness inside my books. I could listen, I could live those worlds—but I couldn't change things.

I found out that meat is animals and felt betrayed; what else were they keeping from me? Chicken food and chicken animal I had thought were different entities, like orange fruit and orange color. Funny that I understood and accepted deception in language first, people second.

I began to evade my mother's eye. I needed minimal supervision—I dressed and fed myself, I was no longer liable to crack my head open on the fireplace, I was a good swimmer. My sister hit me and I would ache to hit her back, to mash the life out of her, but one blow returned would mean another and another, so I absorbed them and went to my mother to be martyred. Soon my mother was angrier at me, for whining about it. She was tired of hearing it, she said. I lost my champion. My father would rage, and she would not, could not intercede. *He is an alcoholic. He has a disease.* But I knew of no other diseases that made people mean instead of sick. *I am leaving, I am the hell out of here,* he would warn, and we would weep and plead with him. While I dreamed of running away with my mother, it was somehow unthinkable for him to go. But he would go, he said. How could we expect him to stay with such a bad family—insolent fighting kids, a wife that smarted off? Please, please, we would beg, and at last he would grant us a brief reprieve. But we children would have to learn. *Yes, what? Yes, sir. You aren't crying, are you? No, sir, my eyes are just watering. Well, then, I'm going to give you something to cry about.*

I got bigger and started to hit back, and my sister called a sullen truce. I learned to anticipate my father's anger and creep furtively to my room. Hide until the threat passed. My mother coped in her own mysterious way, and we seemed to lose track of each other.

I had a set of books called Life Cycle, four slender red volumes with watercolor paintings of testicles, ovaries, babies in the womb. One book outlined what I believed would be my teenage social life. Little buds of breasts rounding out the top of my dress would send a clear, unmistakable signal to boys. They would obtain my phone number and, after a series of nervous conversations, arrange to take me to dinner and a movie. Several dates later, it would be permissible to kiss, and some teenagers might go so far as to "neck and pet," though with extreme caution and only through layers of clothing. Only husbands and wives engaged in that clinical, inexplicable act, also rendered in watercolor, with labeled cross-sections of the organs involved.

I read about hope chests in a magazine for teenage girls and was given one. With my allowance, I bought coasters in anticipation of polished wood surfaces, candles in case mood lighting was someday necessary, wee brass trinkets, sachets. I wrapped them in tissue, the good kind (floral patterned, facial quality), which I used in tandem with Scotch tape to make ball gowns of tulle and voile for my Barbies, harem veils because there were so many of them and only one Ken! Now that hope chest sits in a guest room, filled with headless dolls and mildewed quilts. When I actually became a teenager, hope in general and hope chests in particular were ridiculous. Such was the tyranny of high school.

High school. My new girlfriends and I regaled each other with tales of sex damage culled from our parents' outdated marriage manuals and clandestine porn, from late-night cable TV, from accounts of friends of friends' sisters and cousins, and our own freshly painful penetrations and woe, pap smears and date rapes, still tender, raw, and seeping. A mythology of cautionary tales emerged.

The boy dubbed Dagger Dick, whose abnormally long organ pierced a girl's cervix until she bled to death. The vagina that seized up into an unyielding grip, fusing two bodies as surely stuck and frantic as dogs coupling in the middle of the road. Both heaped onto a stretcher, blanketed and whisked to the emergency room, where the nurses clucked their tongues mildly, having seen worse, or better: anuses clenched around shattered lightbulbs, smothering hamsters, blanching vegetables.

The Freudian power of every tapered and cylindrical thing—a lipstick, a fountain pen, a thimble, all objects to be lost inside. Tampons inserted and forgotten, inserted and forgotten. Pubic hair coiled and dense with crabs. The gag reflex triggered by fellatio, bowels loosed in cunnilingus. Lesions wet and winking tears of blood and pus.

The diligent sperm scrabbling up the virgin's thigh. The teenage fathers, drunk and fleeting, who sire babies in an awkward plunge and squirt, their come an insubstantial gruel trickling toward our robust, magnetic eggs and finding purchase. Ectopic babies that grow and burst fallopian tubes. Twins that swell against the stomach muscles and split them like a zipper. IUD babies with springs embedded in their hands, cigarette babies womb-stunted and asthmatic, alcohol babies dull and listless, dope babies jonesing, acid babies luminous and limbless, failed abortions fist-shaped clumps in the belly. Babies born with teeth in their mouths, cauls over their tong-dented heads, born out of labor that cracks the pelvis and cleaves open the labia; the placenta that refuses to come, sending hemorrhage. Babies born to suck the poison from cancer-studded breasts.

It is a wonder that we dared to have sex at all, but since we did, it is a wonder that we dared do it without multiple barriers of toxic foam, galvanized condoms, and double doses of estrogen. But since we did, it is a wonder we could do it without flinching and nightmares. But this was the nightmare: not being loved. Being a dangling half-being, while everywhere yins and yangs were coiling into perfect circles.

I might share the details of a seduction with friends, but I would omit that the overriding sensation was profound hollowness. How instinctively my legs would part, not from desire but from a perceived necessity. *Conjoin.* It took a long time to get over my astonishment that it could mean next to nothing. The embarrassing intimacy of nakedness could be forgotten in the context of daylight, of school. I would not let on that this bothered me. Nonchalance was the rule for single girls. Only the girls with official boyfriends, publicly confirmed—they appeared together, fingers entwined through one another's belt loops—could cry over the twin mysteries of sex and love. The rest of us acted as if it was all too familiar and a tad dull. Nothing would chase off a potential mate quicker than the scent of desperation.

It took time to get to that stage. My first "lover" had been a boy who came to my house, necked with me for about five minutes, then suggested casually: "Why don't we get out of these clothes?" My response had been visceral and immediate: "I'm a virgin." What a charged word, *virgin.* I was new to understanding what it meant. I had played Mary in our church's reenactment of the nativity. She was a virgin for having a baby by God instead of Joseph. Queen Elizabeth was a virgin. An older boy who lived across the street used to tease me and my friends by saying, "Hello, virgins!" every time he encountered us. I knew and didn't know what a virgin was until the first real threat of invasion. The word and its implications coalesced at the moment of utterance. I had not been out of my clothes, casually or otherwise, with anyone.

I steeled myself for further onslaught. None came. He promptly backed off, gave me a few disinterested kisses, and left. At first I felt relieved, but later I was offended. Uncertain. Was I not a worthwhile conquest? I felt foolish. The boy himself was no prize—a scrawny stoner with dull eyes. It had been his good-looking friend I was interested in, but the good-looking friend had not come over; *he* had. I was making the best of a less than ideal situation. How dare he not be intrigued and bent with desire?

Back at school, he acted cool—not rude, just infuriatingly casual. I decided that this virginity was of no value and that I would discard it at the earliest opportunity. Equally casual, I penned him a note that promised we could give it a go. He came over. We shrugged off our Levi's. His chest was small and bony, like a child's. I kept my shirt on. Intercourse pinched and snagged, but no blood. A mess, still. I blotted and blotted with tissue. We smoked cigarettes because you were supposed to. But what was it I had lost? Still locked tight inside my body was a dense, impenetrable seed of fear and longing.

"I want to go on the Pill," I told my mother, the first thing I had told her in a long, long time, and I watched the new pain darken her face. It was no small satisfaction.

MISSING WOMEN

Three women have vanished—a mother, her teenage daughter, and the daughter's friend—purses and cars left behind, TV on, door unlocked. The daughter had plans to spend the day at the lake with friends and never showed. The phone has rung and rung all morning, unanswered. Puzzled friends walk through the interrupted house, sweep up broken glass from a porch light before calling the police. Broom bristles, shoe soles, finger pads smearing, tamping down, obscuring possibilities. Neighbors come forward, vague. It was late, they say. A green van, a white truck, seen in the area, trolling. A man with longish brown hair, army jacket, slight to medium build. Down by the train tracks, panties. A single canvas sneaker.

Details are not clues. What happened? Police conjecture an intruder or intruders intended only to deal with the mother, to rob or to rape. The girls' arrival was unexpected. Panicking, the perpetrator or perpetrators abducted all three. Haste should have made the abductor or abductors sloppy, dribbling evidence all the way to some lair. But little is found: a single drop of blood in the foyer, but it belongs to a friend—she nicked her finger sweeping up broken glass. We're aghast at all the friends who tidied up. No alarm in broken glass? Those purses; women don't leave their purses.

There is truth and there is rumor. The missing daughter, Vicki, has not been particularly close to the missing friend, Adelle, since junior high. They went in different directions— the stocky, glossy Vicki somewhat of a party girl, her hair bleached yellow-white against iodine skin; Adelle the more academic and wholesomely cheerleaderish one, willowy and fine-boned. Graduation-party nostalgia brought them back together that night, when they let bygones be bygones, forgiving the small betrayals. Adelle called home to say she'd be spending the night at Vicki's house, the first time in almost four years. Her shiny compact car blocks the driveway to show she made it as far as that.

In her abandoned purse is medicine Adelle must take every day. Early on, this is what worries her parents most. They circle the town doggedly, their station wagon filled with flyers, her face emblazoned on their sweatshirts. *Please. If you know anything, anything at all.* In a video they lend to the TV stations, she is modeling gauzy, diaphanous wedding gowns for a local dressmaker. With her skirts and hair swirling, her perfect pearly teeth, we feel that she is innocent and doomed.

Of the missing mother, Kay, and daughter, Vicki, we are not so sure. Their estranged husband/father cannot immediately be located. Vicki's ex-boyfriend once had a restraining order against him and is taken in for questioning. He is at first sullen and uncooperative with investigators. With grim confidence we await his confession, but he foils us: a punched time card and a security video corroborate his third-shift presence in the chicken-parts processing plant that night. The husband/father likewise disappoints. He is not on the lam but simply lives out of state. Someone calls him and he comes, and the son/brother too. They are briefly suspicioned, then cleared. But there is another shady matter. Kay ran a beauty parlor with increasingly disreputable ties. Some say she laundered money for drug dealers and got greedy, funneling too large a share for herself. The police deny all this, but we note her expensive tastes, the leather in her daughter's wardrobe, and conclude the worst.

Still, each of the three might have had her own reasons for wanting to disappear. Kay had maxed out her credit cards and was falling behind in her mortgage payments. Was Vicki pregnant? Some say police found an unopened urine test kit in her bureau. Adelle, the consummate perfectionist, was failing precalculus. Running off might have been easier to contemplate as a group: the girls plotting new looks in better towns; mother Kay mulling over the practical details of bus tickets and low-profile jobs. We cannot rule out anything, but the strongest current is foul play, not the gentle fantasy of escape that we all have entertained.

Seventy-two hours pass without a trace, and the search kicks into high gear. Divers slick in neoprene suits bob the shallow lake as if for apples, rake the algaed muck along the bottom. City workers sonar the reservoir. The waters yield nothing, but the surrounding woods still swarm promisingly with hunters and hounds. We admire these hunters who have volunteered to don their orange caps and peer through binoculars, their dogs fanning out ahead and weaving through trees, loyal noses snuffling the ground. We admire the highway patrolmen in their thin summer khakis, poised in the roadside gravel, dogged but polite at the roadblocks, checking licenses. The churchwomen bring pies and fried chicken and cold cans of soda to everyone tired and hungry from searching, and we admire them too.

All of us admirable, the way we rally together. We say "we." We say "our community," "our women," basking in the evidence of so many heroes lured out by tragedy: storefronts papered by high school kids with flyers provided free by local printshops, reward donations quietly accruing, information streaming through the phone lines, the cards and letters of commiseration. Surely this abundance of goodwill, mercy, and blatant, selfless volunteerism will prevail over the darker elements that abide here. For there are certain haggard people on the street, there are certain small pockets of immigrants who will not master our grammar, whose children are insolent and fearless. There are certain people who look and sound uncannily like the rest of us, but if you shine a light in their crawl spaces you might find the difference. Any might have stared with longing and hatred into the bright windows of pretty blondes.

There are leads. A reporter gets an anonymous call about a box hidden in the park, containing information about the missing women. The caller will not disclose the nature of this information, will not linger on the line. Police are dispatched to the park, locate said box nestled amid gazebo shrubbery, examine it for explosives, dust it for prints, pry it open to find: a map, hastily sketched, of a floor plan. A park official recognizes the U shape of the building, the tiny hexagonal kitchen and bathroom appendages flanking individual units. Police converge on the apartment building. Excited tenants cluster in the halls as rooms are searched. Nothing. *Wild Goose Chase*, go the headlines. *Police Vexed by Fruitless Search*. Again Adelle's parents appear on television. Their anguish chastens other would-be pranksters, but was it just a prankster? Someone who could snatch three women away without a trace might then goad the searchers. No person of authority will come right out and say so, but there it is. We feel it, huddled indoors or venturing out in twos and threes.

A Waffle Hut waitress comes forward. She is fairly certain she served the three women omelets, French toast, and coffee around two A.M. on the morning of the disappearance. They seemed quietly anxious, not like the raucous post-bar crowd she usually waits on around that time. The cheerleader type asked for boysenberry syrup, and when told there was none, sank into a sullen lassitude.

A SuperDairy QuikMart clerk comes forward. Around two A.M. on the morning of the disappearance, a woman resembling the missing mother burst into the store abruptly, asked if he had seen two teenage girls, and stormed out when he said he hadn't. She sometimes bought cigarettes there, and milk in single-serving containers.

The graduation party attendees are questioned further. The two girls were spotted leaving the party together variously at one A.M., two A.M. and three A.M. The hostess thought she heard them arguing in the bathroom, something about a borrowed necklace. The hostess's parents said both girls were polite and charming but seemed troubled. The hostess's boyfriend saw them hugging on the lawn. Others said the lawn embrace was a brawl; Vicki had Adelle in a choke hold. Or Adelle held Vicki while she vomited malt liquor onto the zinnias. Unless it wasn't those two at all. The salutatorian has his doubts. At around one-thirty A.M., he says, he was sitting alone on the back patio. He had turned down a joint, only to have the smoke blown into his ear, leaving him giddy and fretful and confused. He is going to Yale in the fall, and the prospect was then lying heavily on his mind. Now he feels relief and a delightful anticipation of leaving, but that night he brooded while the full moon silhouetted two figures dancing together on the lawn. The salutatorian watched in darkness two moving bodies he could identify as female only by their shapes, the pitch of their laughter. It's possible they kissed or merely whispered. He is pale and stammering in recall. Police seize his journals but return them the very next day, almost dejected. His nervous intelligence seemed so promising—a budding sociopath?—but his journals hold only the sex-obsessed ramblings of run-of-the-mill adolescence: "May 5—Would absolutely rut Bethany R. given half a chance. Tits like grapefruit and she smells like bubble-gum-flavored suntan lotion and sex."

The time is ripe for confessions, so people start to confess, as if in fits of misguided volunteerism. Some march right into the police station or the newspaper editor's office. Some hold press conferences. A man calling himself a freelance private eye and soldier of fortune says he helped the women conceal their identities and relocate, to where he is forbidden to disclose, but rest assured they are alive and well, enjoying lucrative careers in finance. A youth generally regarded as troubled leads police and reporters to an empty culvert, a deserted rail car, and on a hike through acres of abandoned field. Someone claiming actually to be one of the missing women comes forward but will not specify which one she is—she resembles none—and is vague about the other two, saying only that they ditched her. Her parents convince her to recant. A group calling itself The Urban Tide says they have taken the women hostage in belated protest of the U.S. invasion of Grenada. They are revealed to be performance artists living off college fellowships. They say their intention was to "tweak the media and thereby tweak collective perceptions." There is talk of dismantling the university's theater arts program altogether, which is hotly debated until the diversion of Vicki's ex-boyfriend's appearance in a television interview.

He reaffirms his innocence and describes their first date: They had agreed to meet at the football game. She had not permitted him to kiss her that night. The first thing he admired about her was how she blew smoke rings, "like she was forty years old or something." They dated for two years and got pre-engaged. She loved red hots and for him to knead her shoulders after a long day of school and sweeping up at her mother's shop. The restraining order grew out of a misunderstanding, he explains. He was a jealous guy, he admits. She could be sort of a flirt, but no more than that, he is careful to emphasize. No speaking ill of the missing. He has grown up a lot since then, he swears, and in a pretaped clip, his former guidance counselor agrees. What's next for this wrongly accused young fellow who has stolen all our hearts? He's studying for his General Equivalency Diploma and plans to enter technical school. Weekends he fishes with his dad and brothers.

Lovely Adelle had (has? We must be careful with what tenses imply) no boyfriend. She seemed unapproachable, schoolmates say. Boys were intimidated by her height and her perfect smile. She carried herself as if maybe she thought she was a little better than everyone else. We detect the trace of a smugly superior smirk in her wedding dress video. Her parents start to seem a little *too* perfect in their televised worry, forever circling the town, meeting with the police chief, presiding over candlelight vigils. We can't help but wonder: Don't they have to work? The friendly wood panels on their station wagon begin to come across as less than sincere. When Adelle's face appears alone on a billboard and a separate award fund is established from her college savings, we say they are elitist. Someone rents a billboard featuring only the faces of the other two, and passers-through unfamiliar with the case think they are unrelated disappearances.

The paper still presents them as a united front, the Missing Women, and prints their photos side by side in equal rectangles. The rectangles have shrunk in size, though, and are delegated to the B pages except on Sundays, when a summary appears on the front page, featuring the best of the tip cards and the psychic du jour. In the absence of verifiable fact, reporters track the psychics' emanations and contribute wispy, artful meditations on the nature of truth itself. One reporter suggests that the women never really existed at all except as modern local archetypes: Kay the divorced mom, Vicki the short-skirted slattern, Adelle the model child from a better neighborhood. Cruise any strip mall in town, he muses, and you will see several of their ilk. Subscriptions to the paper take a nosedive until the reporter resigns and a larger-format, full-color TV schedule is introduced.

How we are holding up: summer presses on, August flares. As the ringing phones wane, crime line volunteers drop off reluctantly, like rose petals. Friends and relatives of the missing women who have flocked to town must return to their respective homes, more immediate families, jobs. There is no such thing as indefinite leave unless you are the missing women. Flyers in windows start to flap at the edges, tape losing its tack. Still, church attendance remains up. Moonlight strolls are kept to a minimum. Locksmiths can't install deadbolts quickly enough. Neighborhoods stay illuminated by floodlights and seethe with attack dogs. Psychologists from the university advise us, in these prolonged times of stress, to be absolutely forthright with one another and to get plenty of rest and light-to-moderate exercise. Sixty-four percent of residents polled believe there will be more disappearances. Seventy-nine percent say the missing women are dead. Eleven percent believe that the supernatural was involved. Two percent suggest they know something about the disappearance that the rest of us don't, and they aren't telling. The poll has a two percent margin of error.

Our police chief is often spotted raking his hand though thin, whitening hair, loosening his collar. He has gained thirty pounds. We worry that the ordeal will force him into early retirement. Mostly we appreciate what he has done for the town, keeping both the leftist fringe and the religious zealots at bay to preserve our moderate sensibilities. Whereas our mayor is perceived to be an ineffectual weasel, the apprehended drunk drivers, college rowdies, neo-Nazis, drug dealers, and other assorted riffraff can attest that our police chief has kept the peace. But even he cannot collar this invisible threat to our women, this thief who whisks them away into the night, leaving only their plaintive flat faces pressed against yellowing planes of paper, asking everyone: Have you seen us?

August simmering down, the newspaper finally succumbs to investigative inertia. No news is no news; they've been carrying the missing women for weeks now, without a single new development. Journalism must prevail; the women's photos are stricken from the B pages. Without the newspaper's resolve, we let the county fair distract us, then a strike at the chicken-parts processing plant, then the college students coming back to town. There's talk of rebuilding the stadium. We have our hands full.

The mayor orates, finally. This tragedy has torn at the heart of our community, he says. We are shocked, saddened, and bewildered, he says. Grappling for clues. Desperate for answers. Neighbor pitted against neighbor in suspicion and fear. We are momentarily tensed by the drama of his speech, but he is voicing sentiments of weeks ago. A belated coda. We've gotten on with it. That's his problem: no finger on the pulse. He's slow to evaluate, even slower to act. We resent his jowly, bowtied demeanor. He proposes a monument in the square, a small gas torch that will stay lit, eternally vigilant, until the women return. Donations trickle in, guiltily.

From this, the newspaper enjoys a brief second wind of missing-women coverage. After the press conference, there are additional quotes to be gleaned from the mayor, the locally available friends and family of the missing, and the major contributors to the gas torch. There is even a statement from the fire marshal, attesting to the relative safety of the proposed monument. The newspaper's cartoonist, known for her acid social commentary, calls attention to the downtown homeless by drawing bums and bag ladies toasting skewered rats over the torch's open flame. It is generally derided as tasteless, and the editor prints what amounts to an apology under Corrections, saying "We regret the error." The cartoonist resigns under pressure and files suit. She donates part of her settlement to the torch fund, part to the soup kitchen. There will be other, occasional flare-ups. Adelle's parents will reemerge woefully from time to time, but in retrospect we will see that it was here the story's last traces turned to ash.

And what of the missing women? They do turn up, but only in dreams. We're at a party, and though the dream seems intended to air private anxieties (we find ourselves naked in a room full of people), there are the three of them, lingering over the bean dip. Or we walk into an alcove filled with light, to see Adelle in her wedding dress, spinning, spinning, her face aging with each rotation, the smile lined and straining, g-forces undulating her cheeks. Or from the reception area of her beauty shop, we watch Kay cutting hair that drops in soft heaps, the yellow-blond hair of her daughter, black at the root. Or the girls are wearing graduation caps and robes and clutching scrolls. The scrolls are not diplomas but maps of their whereabouts. They offer us a peek, but when we lean in to look, they pull away, snickering with teenage disdain, and vanish. Or in the one we don't speak of, we are running down a familiar forest path, hunted, and we sense them beneath the pads of our feet, planted deep in the dark green woods, bones cooling, and we wake, knowing they've been here all along.

June Spence's stories have appeared in *The Best American Short Stories 1997, The Southern Review, Seventeen,* and *The Oxford American.* The winner of the 1995 Willa Cather Award, she lives in Raleigh, North Carolina, where she was born.